Richard Burleigh Kimball

Henry Powers (Banker)

How He Achieved a Fortune, and Married

Richard Burleigh Kimball

Henry Powers (Banker)
How He Achieved a Fortune, and Married

ISBN/EAN: 9783337001186

Printed in Europe, USA, Canada, Australia, Japan

Cover: Foto ©Andreas Hilbeck / pixelio.de

More available books at **www.hansebooks.com**

HENRY · POWERS,

(Banker.)

How He Achieved a Fortune, and Married.

A Novel.

By RICHARD B. KIMBALL,

AUTHOR OF

"SAINT LEGER,"—"ROMANCE OF STUDENT LIFE,' —
"WAS HE SUCCESSFUL?"
"UNDERCURRENTS,"—
&c., &c., &c.

"There is a tide in the affairs of men, which, taken at the flood, leads on to fortune."—JULIUS CÆSAR.

NEW YORK:

G. W. Carleton & Co., Publishers,

LEIPSIC: TAUCHNITZ.

MDCCCLXVIII.

DEDICATED

TO

WILLIAM B. SHATTUCK, ESQ.,

TO WHOM THE AUTHOR IS
INDEBTED FOR THE IDEA OF THIS BOOK.

R B K

CONTENTS.

CHAPTER XV.

CHAPTER XVI.

CHAPTER XVII.

CHAPTER XVIII

CHAPTER XIX.

CHAPTER XX.

CHAPTER XXI.

CHAPTER XXII.

HENRY POWERS, BANKER.

HOW HE

ACHIEVED A FORTUNE, AND MARRIED.

CHAPTER I.

IN one of the large marble structures which have lately been erected in Nassau Street, between Cedar and Wall Streets, there is, on the first floor above the basement, a fine suite of rooms, fitted up for what in America is termed a banking house—in Europe it would be called a commercial house; but this matters little to my history. The rooms have the appearance of being solidly and substantially employed. There is no gleam of varnish or fresh paint about them. The

clerks are numerous; every one is quietly ab-
sorbed in his duties.

The real condition of the firm which occu-
pies this floor (unlike that of many in New York
which I could name if I felt inclined) does not
belie the promising features which the apartments display. The New Yorker will at once
agree with me, when I add that I am speaking
of the house of Powers & Holman.

Reader, I am Henry Powers, the senior partner.

What should induce me to give this account
of myself? My standing in financial circles
throughout the country, indeed over Europe,
where my operations are extensive and my cir-
cular letters of credit gladly honored, is too
firmly established to require explanation. My
wife's position in society is so assured, that there
is no movement of any importance, from the benevolent scheme of a charity ball to the opening
of the last fashionable race-course, in which she
does not figure.

It is not then from any desire for greater distinction or notoriety that I indulge the public. Possibly the best reason I can give, is that "it is my humor." The summer is approaching. The gay world and the traveling world, want something to interest them as they pass to and fro, while the student and the philosopher are not at times disinclined to relaxation or to taking a leaf out of such a book as mine. Perhaps they may do so and be all the wiser for it.

I dare say my financial friends, and my fashionable friends will consider this a work of fiction. I shall not attempt to disabuse them, but I assure my out-of-town readers, with seriousness, that this story is true, every word of it, from the avowal of the name of my banking firm in Nassau Street to the minutest detail here recorded.

A work of fiction, indeed! That would not become the gravity of my position before the world. No. I leave novel writing to "the reverend the clergy" who are now invading this last bomb-proof of the "legitimate" author, turning his own guns against him; appropriating all his stock in trade and leaving him helpless. Were it not that I do not wish to seem even to treat with levity things which I consider sacred, I would advise writers of romance, in their turn, to rush to the pulpit, which they would, perchance find empty, and undertake to do duty there. A fair exchange, and one, perhaps, quite to the satisfaction of their hearers.

Having said thus much by way of introducing myself, I will proceed straight to my work. In doing this I must begin at the beginning.

CHAPTER II.

I was born near a small village on the Connecticut River, in New Hampshire. Not precisely under the shadow of the White Mountains, but where they were distinctly visible in the distance. There is no lovelier scenery in the world than that of the valley of the Connecticut. As you advance northward, it becomes more grand and impressive, until the majestic range which culminates in Mount Washington appears in view. Our city-bred people know but little of the hardy, vigorous life which the inhabitants lead. And I fear I should not interest them if I attempted to describe it.

My father was a man in delicate health. He owned a small farm of about thirty acres, which with good cultivation and a careful economy served to support my father, my mother, and myself.

Continued ill health had softened and refined my father's character. He was thoughtful and considerate, and differed much from the farmers in the neighborhood. He was fond of reading, and not being able to work all the time, he indulged his taste for it. He cultivated the soil with intelligent industry, so that our thirty acres produced as much as some farms of one hundred. My mother had a sanguine, happy-tempered, joyous nature, and made our little household always cheerful. She was not intellectual, but she had a keen shrewd sense of the fitness of things. I was an only child, and · grew up more as a companion than any thing else. Those were happy days as I now recall them: "Us three," as we used to say, forming the entire family. We lived a life of perfect independence. Thirty years ago, manners were much more primitive in that district than now. There were no railroads in the vicinity to connect us closely with the large towns. The stage performed its daily route, not ordinarily

more than half filled with passengers, and all
the news we obtained was gleaned from the
weekly paper. I attended the "district school"
with the other children of the neighborhood. In
the winter it was kept by a schoolmaster, in
the summer by a schoolmistress, because then
all the large boys were at work in the fields
and none but girls and small boys were in attendance. My father took a great deal of pains
to make me like my books, and my mother
used to hear my spelling lesson every morning
before I started for school, to be sure I had
learned it correctly. By these aids and that of
close application and a good memory I kept at
the head of all my classes, and acquired the
reputation of being a very bright boy. After
I was thirteen I no longer attended in the summer, and at sixteen I quitted the district school
altogether.

There was an excellent academy in the large
village about three miles from our house, to which
my father concluded to send me in order that I

might obtain, as he said, a first-rate English education. He could not well afford to pay my board there, but it was decided that I should live at home and attend as a day scholar. In fine weather I used to walk both ways—when the weather was stormy, my father drove me over and back.

Thus far I had formed no plans for my future. I did not, indeed, expect to confine myself to the little thirty-acre farm. I had a vague ambitious thought of making a great deal of myself, but this was not at all defined. It had assumed no tangible shape. It was airy, romantic, unsubstantial, not connected with any idea of severe work, or of surmounting difficulties or enduring hardships. The fact is, I had really but a slight notion of the busy world that throbbed feverishly in our great cities, or what was going on there. So every thing was left to my imagination, and that, as you all know, plays strange freaks with serious sober fact.

At the academy, however, I gained a good deal

besides what I learned from my studies. Intercourse with the boys and young men, who came from different parts of New England, was of great service. My horizon began speedily to enlarge, and continued to expand. I was confessedly the smartest boy at the district school. Indeed, I had no competitor who approached me.

At the academy I met young fellows every way my equal in capacity, who had many advantages which I had not enjoyed. This stimulated me to greater exertion, and brought ambition for the first time fully into action. Here, too, I began to see and appreciate the power of money. It was at first a mysterious agency not easily to be understood by my unsophisticated mind. I did not at first comprehend the force of the magic words, when some one would say of one of the boys, " His father is very rich !" or of another, " He is poor—he is a charity scholar." I do not mean to be understood that there were at this school any thing like aristocratic cliques, or invidious distinctions, but there was always enough to draw my

attention to the fact, that the world worships
wealth.   This conviction roused a throng of feelings within me.   I determined to be rich.

Before this I had regarded with some envy
the class of young men who were fitting for col-
lege.   I think, had I asked my father's consent
to endeavor to obtain a classical -education, he
would have granted it; but with my new views
(I confess it now with shame), I considered that
this would not be the quickest or surest road to
a fortune, and I decided not to take it.   Not
to go further into the details of my school life,
I continued at the academy nearly four years.
In that time I had mastered all that was taught
there pertaining to an English education, and had
gained the position of the "best scholar" in that
department.   I left with the highest testimonials
from the principal, which I exhibited to my father
and mother with an honest pride.

CHAPTER III.

I was now to begin life. For a week I suffered from a vague irresolution. A rather singular circumstance decided my course and that suddenly. When I made up my mind to try above all things to make money, I concluded to enter on some commercial pursuit as the best way of doing it. In the large village where I had been studying were two or three first-class stores, where I could readily find a place to commence my business experience before undertaking a higher flight. I had not yet applied to either, but was hesitating in my choice.

I have purposely omitted to make an avowal of which I need not feel ashamed, since in the course of nature it overtakes everybody. I was in love, or at least I thought I was.

Emma Parks was the daughter of the wealthiest man in our vicinity. He lived in the small

village which was near our house, and had a fine
place. He owned two or three farms in the
county, and occupied himself in various ways.
He had been a contractor on the railroad, and
thus made a considerable sum. He was in the
habit of buying droves of cattle, and sending
them to market; he would invest money in wool,
and sell or hold it as he thought best.   In this
way he was kept very active, and more than half
his time from home; and when he was with his
family, he paid little attention to what was going
on in domestic matters.   His wife was a pleasant
lady; not in very good health.   They had two
children, both daughters.   The eldest, Emma,
scarcely a year younger than myself, the other a
child of ten or twelve years old.

There was but one church, or " meeting-house,"
as it was called, in the small village, where all
gathered together on Sundays: the hard-working
farmers and children to doze through the long
tedious sermon, the young men and women to
look very grave and think of each other, leaving

an exemplary few to pay a serious attention to the discourse, and profit by it if possible.

I had known Emma Parks ever since I could remember. We were at the district school together, she was in my class and my closest competitor. This brought us next to each other as we stood up to read or spell, and while I was generally at the head, she was quite sure to be next. I recollect well that if unfortunately she missed in a word and lost her place I felt lonely till she regained it, which she was sure speedily to do, and when she stood again by my side I experienced a pleasure which I knew she shared with me. Once I was detected in "telling," that is, in assisting her to answer a question, a grave offense, for which I had to take my place at the foot. It was some satisfaction to me that it gave Emma the head, but the distance between us seemed a thousand miles. It was a week before I could reascend to the position next her. The boys and girls tried hard, I think, to keep me down, by getting their les-

2

sons better than usual.   Emma said nothing, but I felt that she experienced a glow of delight when I finally reached my place.

Two years after, Emma was sent to a female seminary in the southern part of the State, and I went to the academy. We saw very little of each other till she returned from school to be at home. I had still a year to remain where I was. I never knew any one change so little as Emma, except that she had attained her full size, and looked like a young lady instead of a child. She treated me precisely as if she had not been away at all, and with her old partiality.

I was, as I have said, still at the academy, with one more year before me. We had there a debating society, which met on Saturday afternoon, and to which the public were admitted. Emma never missed an opportunity to be present, and when the season was fine we walked leisurely back the whole three miles together. These miles seemed very short, indeed a mere stroll. The punctuality with which both of us attended the evening lectures was most remarkable. Yet not altogether inexplicable, when I tell you that after the services were over, I always was Emma's attendant home, to reach which we generally took a long detour. Once I recollect missing her in the crowd as it pressed out of the door. I was in despair; in vain I looked in every direction, I had given up all hope of meeting her that evening and was starting on my way home, when I caught sight of her at a little distance, evidently waiting for me. She quietly put her arm in mine, and without either saying one word we walked on.

I can not describe the state of ecstasy I was in through all that year. It gave me fresh strength, I studied the harder for it, and grew the more ambitious to make money. Everybody said Emma Parks would be rich. I resolved I would never speak to her of marriage, I would not seek to be engaged, I would never even say I loved her until *I* was rich. I felt assured of *her* love in return, for how else could all

these tokens be explained? Besides, she showed
no favor to any of the young men in the neighborhood. Indeed it would seem by their conduct
that they had left the field entirely to me.

There was one thing alone, only one thing,
which caused me any distress.

On a fine Sunday morning, two or three
months after Emma's return from the seminary,
I saw a genteely dressed and rather good-look-
ing young man in her father's pew. There
should be nothing very astonishing in that,
though Mr. Parks was at that time away from
home.

I felt jealous of the stranger, I hardly knew
why. He was very polite to Mrs. Parks, but not
specially so to Emma. The next morning he had
vanished. I heard no one allude to him, as is
common frequently in coming out of church, and
for some reason I was reluctant to make any
inquiry.

Emma and I met as usual at the lecture-room,
Thursday evening. No allusion was made to the

young man who had occupied her pew. Her
manner was as kind as ever, our walk longer, so
that I laughed at myself for feeling as I had
done over so trivial an occurrence.

But it was repeated! Several weeks after,
when the affair had gone quite out of my mind,
the specter, in the shape of that identical stranger, appeared again. This time I was more fortunate in getting information. The clergyman's
wife, coming out, said in a low tone to the wife
of one of the deacons, "That's the gentleman
Emma Parks is engaged to." "Who is he?"
was asked. "Dr. Emory, from Andover."

I was so wedged in the crowd that I could
not fail to hear this, and, although I know I
turned very red, it did not affect me as much
as one would suppose. The affair was so over-
stated that I felt a sort of relief. "Andover!"
That was where Emma had been at school.
What wonder people should fall in love with
her. Surely she can not prevent that. Besides,
I recalled the fact that the Parks family had con-

nections in Andover by the name of Emory;
and here was one of them. So, when I heard
the same statement repeated outside the church
door, I said to myself, "Ha! ha! How little
they know of what is between Emma Parks and
me!" In fact I rather enjoyed the common
mistake of the congregation.

Nevertheless I felt impatient for Thursday
evening to come. I thought I might venture a
joke about the current opinion. Then we could
enjoy the little affair together. But when the
evening did come, and when, after impatiently
sitting through an unusually long lecture, I found
myself once more by Emma, her arm in mine,
her hand in mine, walking very slowly, as we
were wont, I had not the courage nor yet the
inclination to disturb, by such an allusion, the
placid, the perfect happiness we were mutually
enjoying.

Thus matters went on till I left the academy.

On the day of the "Exhibition" which marked
the close of the term, and which was held in the

largest church of the village, Emma attended and
occupied a conspicuous place in the gallery set
aside for ladies. As I went on the "stage," at
the conclusion of the day's proceedings, to receive
by public announcement the first prize, I ventured to cast a glance in the direction where she
was sitting. I did not trust myself to do so before.

She was looking toward me intently, but
turned her eyes quickly away as they met mine.
In a few minutes we were together, taking our
walk homeward of three miles.

It was a lovely day in September. In this
locality the foliage changes early into innumerable
colors without falling off. The appearance of the
forests was magnificent and aided to produce a
dreamy, delightful sentiment. Lest our walk
should come too quickly to its close we turned
into an old road, leading in the same direction,
formerly in use but now quite deserted

On this occasion Emma talked more than
usual. She spoke of her gratification at the honors I had gained, and asked me what I was now

going to do. She had never before said any thing to me on the subject. I told her I intended to enter on a commercial pursuit. I was uncertain where to commence, but thought I should go to Boston in a few days, and on my return decide between that city and one of the larger stores here.

"Boston is a long way from here," she said hesitating; "besides, don't you think it would be better to become a little familiar with business before you go to so large a place?"

She spoke in a lower tone than usual, and I fancied—only fancied—I could perceive the slightest possible pressure of her arm in mine. What a subtle, mysterious power have the sex! I determined that instant I would begin my career not in Boston but in the large village near by.

I did not say so though. I only said, "Perhaps you are right," and the conversation was changed. We made very slow progress toward home. Indeed, it was not till the setting sun admonished us to quicken our steps that I remembered we had still more than a mile to walk.

CHAPTER IV.

YES, now I was to begin! and, as I have stated in the opening of the last chapter, I was by no means resolved where. It was Emma Parks who determined me not to go at once to the city, but to commence my career nearer home. On Thursday evening I should see her, and I would then talk with her fully about my plans. On that evening I went as usual to the lecture. Emma was not there! Who can describe the agony of my impatience as I was forced to sit out those tedious services, and go home alone. I imagined every thing. I scarcely slept that night. I tried to reason myself into a calmer state. "What occasion for such an excitement of feeling," I said half aloud. "Emma has been kept at home by some unforeseen circumstance. Am I to go through life in this way, nervous and

2*

full of fears at the least disappointment! Nonsense!"

I was not very successful in the attempt to quiet myself. Still I devoted the next day to the consideration of the best store for me to enter in the large village. I thought the next morning I would walk over and talk with the owner of one of these. I had just breakfasted, and was about starting on this errand when there was a rap at the door. My mother opened it. I was in the adjoining room. When I came out she had just finished the reading of a note she held in her hand. She had another which she gave me. Saying, "Well, it has come at last." I took the prettily folded bit of paper without a misgiving. Opening it, I read as follows:

"Mr. and Mrs. Parks request the pleasure of Mr. Henry Powers's company on Monday evening, at the wedding of their daughter."

I did not turn red or pale. But it seemed as if my soul was suddenly changed to stone.

My mother did not appear to notice me, but said, "They were going to be married when Emma first came home from school, but it was put off." "Yes," was my reply, as if I knew all about it, and not a word more was uttered. The next day, Sunday, I attended church as usual, and saw, of course, Dr. Emory seated in Mr. Parks's pew next to Emma—my Emma!

Monday evening we attended the wedding. I stood very near and saw them married. Afterward, I congratulated the bride. She received me very sweetly—yes, indeed, and looked her prettiest, as all brides do. I shook hands with the doctor, and gave his fingers a grip that brought the tears to his eyes. During the evening, after the married pair had received all the congratulations of the guests, I walked with Mrs. Emory around the room. She had my arm. I made no allusion whatever to any thing that was passing; nor did she. We talked as we had always talked, and for a little while I felt as if I had been dreaming a horrible dream, and had happily awakened. This last hallucination was soon dissolved. The doctor came up and joined us as we were standing near the mantel-piece. A few common-place words were exchanged, when Emma quietly withdrew her arm from mine and took her husband's. She smiled kindly as she did this, and both walked away.

The company broke up soon after I left. It was not till I reached home and had retired, that a sense of utter desolation came over me.

I did not sleep a wink that night. I made a thousand resolutions, and as quickly abandoned them. I would think no more of this wicked world; no more of entering into business. It was sinful, carnal, diabolical. I would study for the ministry. I would devote myself to doing good. I would become a missionary, and preach the gospel to the far, very far-off heathen. I would sacrifice, yes, crucify myself.

The day dawned while I was still feverishly resolving these lofty views. I lay until the sun began to stream into my window. My door stood ajar. I had omitted to close it when I went to bed. It opened into the kitchen. My mother had been for some time busy in the preparations for breakfast. Soon my father came in and took a seat.

"Is not Henry up yet?" he said.

"No," replied my mother, "I thought I would let him sleep."

"Don't you think, wife," continued my father, after a pause, "that Henry was in love with Emma Parks?"

"In love," exclaimed my mother, while she gave one of her clear ringing good-natured laughs. "In love; nothing but puppy love. It will do him good; it will shake up and settle his sympathies. Boys have to go through with it as they do with the hooping-cough and the measles."

She laughed again as merrily as before, and I fancied I could hear a responsive tone from my father—low and quiet, as was his way.

"Puppy love!" Was this the commentary

on my lofty aspirations, my swelling hopes, my
tumultuous feelings, my tender emotions and
desires! And from my mother, my kind, partial, affectionate mother! "Puppy love!" What
a disagreeable expression. What do my parents
think of me? I fancied my secret so well
kept, and now I saw it was no secret at all.
My clear-sighted, quick-witted mother knew all
about it, and had held her peace, it seems, till
the malady, like the measles, should have its
run. Probably the whole village knew and were
chuckling over it.

How disgusted I was at every thing and everybody. This ebullition passed off. After awhile
pride began to have its proper control. Presently my mother knocked at the door, and said,
"Breakfast is ready." I rose and tried to appear
as if nothing had happened.

We finished the meal. Then I went back to
my room. "No country store for me, no Boston for me, I will strike for the largest place,
and I will make my mark there. I will go to

New York!" This resolve was the result of a day of bitter communing with myself.

    .   .   .   .   .   .

My arrangements were speedily perfected. I should require what seemed to me a very considerable sum of money—thirty-five or forty dollars at least. My father relieved my anxiety on this point. He always had, he said, a little put by for a rainy day; and from this store, which proved to be not quite fifty dollars, I received forty. My mother slipped five in my hand as she bade me farewell, and thus fortified I jumped into the stage which was to convey me about half a day's ride to the nearest railroad station from which I was to be whirled into the great maelstrom of metropolitan life.

Of this life I had not the slightest conception. I had once visited Concord, the capital of my native State, a town of eight or ten thousand inhabitants. It was the largest place I was ever in, and the only one by which I could judge of New York. I could not there-

fore form the least idea of the sharp-cut divi-
sion of labor; the close and eager competition,
the perpetual, unceasing hum of action, and the
ever-varied, never-ending preparatives for pleasure
which characterize the great metropolis. It was
an unknown, untried sea. God help the youth
who first attempts it!

CHAPTER V.

LET me insert a short chapter here in parenthesis. The account I give of my "affair," with Emma Parks is by no means novel. It is the experience of nineteen young fellows out of twenty. Doubtless my mother was right, when she characterized my state of feverish agitation by the term "puppy love." By which expression—rather grating it must be confessed to the youth concerned—I suppose she meant to convey her strong conviction, that the feelings and emotions I entertained had no depth, but were from the surface, and would not stand the test of time and of new scenes, or even the ordinary change of events.

This I now readily comprehend. But what of Emma Parks! Certainly *her* conduct can not be explained in this way. During the entire year, and while she was engaged to the man she subsequently married, she gave me tokens of her affection which I could not mistake, and by her treatment plunged me into the condition I have endeavored to describe.

Yet I can not think she was otherwise than sincere. She had not the disposition of a coquette, nor do I believe she was merely amusing herself by flirting with me. The idea that she had engaged herself rashly, and would have broken off the compact if she could—in short, that she preferred me to Dr. Emory, I must reject. Emma Parks, as everybody well knew, had absolutely her own way at home. Her father indulged her slightest wish, while her mother never thought for a moment of opposing any plan she ever formed. So that her temper was not of a sort to tolerate any restraint on her choice, or prevent her openly avowing any change of mind. I repeat, therefore, the whole affair is to me utterly incomprehensible.

*   *   *   *   *   *   *   *

"What a goose you are," exclaimed my wife, who, while I was a few moments absent from the room, had entered and cast her eyes over the foregoing pages, "what a goose you are!"

"Why?" I asked, in a rather subdued tone, for I felt somewhat ashamed at being caught at my little bit of sentimentality.

"Why?" responded she. "Because you make a mystery of the simplest thing in the world. The girl had been your companion from the time you were children together, and she liked you, and treated you accordingly. But you were the last person she ever would fall in love with. Besides, girls are much more mature than boys, and at nineteen she was ready to be married, when you,"—my wife hesitated and smiled.

"I, what?"

"Well, when you doubtless merited the appellation bestowed by your mother."

"I guess you are right," was my response.

"Set a thief to catch a thief, and a woman to explain a woman."

"My dear," said my wife, "I came to call you to dinner!"

.   .   .   .

CHAPTER VI.

I HAD a single acquaintance in New York. It was a young man by the name of Amos Carter, a relation of one of our neighbors. He had spent a few weeks in our village, the previous summer, and I had become well acquainted with him. He was salesman in a wholesale grocery store, and gave me a warm invitation to come and see him, if I ever visited the city. It occurred to me that I might be assisted in the choice of a boarding-house by this young man, and I resolved to call on him without delay.

I arrived in town by the New Haven Railroad, in the express train, which reaches Twenty-seventh Street about half-past eleven at night, and put up at one of the cheap hotels near the station. I slept soundly, and did not awake till late. It was the first refreshing

slumber I had experienced since the shock which
had so affected me.

I started up, and looked confusedly around.
I was no longer in my neat little chamber
at home, but in a dreary, dirty-looking room,
without furniture of any kind if I may except
a washstand, two chairs, and the bed I was in.
I dressed as quickly as possible, in order to be
rid of the impression produced by the scene,
and hastened down to breakfast. That dispatched,
I made the necessary inquiries for reaching Water
Street, where Mr. Carter was, and started in
search of it.

What a sight for me, as the omnibus passed
down Broadway. I can never forget it, nor
the impression produced by it. It equaled the
"Tales of the Arabian Nights." One wonder
succeeded another, until I felt almost beside
myself.

.   .   .   .

At last I found the place and number. It
was a large building, running through to the

next street. I well recollect the sign over the door. It was, "Embury, Hyde & Prince." Several carts were standing by so as to almost completely block the entrance, and persons were busy loading them. I managed to push my way into the store, and endeavored to find some one sufficiently at leisure to speak to me: but everybody was at work. Not the least notice was taken of my presence. At length I seized a propitious moment, and inquired of a young man if Mr. Carter was in. The only answer he made, was to point with his finger to the interior of the store. I went forward, and asked again. Another point of the finger up-stairs. I ascended and inquired once more and got a word in reply, "Not up here." I retorted, that I had been sent up there. "Went down five minutes ago," was jerked out in answer.

I retraced my steps, and finding the person who had directed me, told him Mr. Carter was not up-stairs. The man stared vacantly at me an instant, then rapidly called out, "Jim, where's Carter?" "Pearl Street door!" was echoed back. Another finger-point toward the Pearl Street entrance, and my man was off.

On I walked, and my perseverance was rewarded. For there was Carter, his coat off (it was a very warm day), busy taking in goods. He recognized me at once, as I presented myself, and shook hands in a manner which indicated he really had not the time to do it; while one eye was kept constantly on the men at the door.

"I'm glad to see you, very glad to see you. Leave all well? Come and see me this evening. Hold on! Let me give you my address."

"Have you any room, do you think—for another boarder?" I was about to ask, when I was suddenly pushed aside, with a "Take care, those grappling-irons will hit you." "Be sure and come up this evening. Come early; don't forget, now. Busy time with us, you see. Good-day."

I had too much sense to be angry at my

reception, for I could see that Carter really *was* busy, and unable to attend to me; but I felt mortified and vexed nevertheless. So I said "Good-day," in return, and started off.

I left the store of Embury, Hyde & Prince, with a rather diminished sense of my own importance. The idea gradually dawned on me that I was not actually necessary to the merchants of New York. I put on a bold front, however, determining not to be faint-hearted. I spent the day riding over the city in the omnibuses and horse-cars, and in the evening presented myself at the place named by Carter as his boarding-house.

Here my reception was quite different from the greeting at the store. Carter was glad to see me; asked me at once to his room, which was a very comfortable apartment, nicely furnished, and where his repose of manner was in strange contrast with the hurry and bustle of the day. I took tea with him, and then told him what I had come to New York for.

3

"I will do what I can for you," he said, "but it is difficult to get a good place—very difficult. We are full at our store—am sure. One thing I can do—I can get you in here. It is an excellent house. The old lady is from New England, and makes us all feel as if we were living at home. There is an attic room vacated to-day, if you don't mind climbing a little. The price is five dollars a week, very reasonable as things are going."

I examined the room, which I reached after what seemed to me an interminable ascent, and which proved to be a small, cramped corner, but clean and neat. Five dollars a week for a seven-by-nine nook in a garret (Carter called it an attic), looked large to me; but I was satisfied it was the best I could do, and that I was fortunate in securing it. So I thanked my friend; and having an intense repugnance to passing another night at the hotel, I inquired if I could not bring my trunk that very evening and install myself at once in my lodgings. There was no objection to this, and accordingly I went back to the scene of the previous night, paid my bill, and hired a porter to carry my luggage to my new home.

I had a long conversation with Carter that evening. He seemed disposed to aid me every way in his power. His suggestions were useful, though I was greatly chagrined to learn I could not step at once into a good situation.

"You have no acquaintances here, then," said he, after considerable discussion.

"None but yourself."

"Well, never mind," he continued, "I will introduce you to one of our firm, and from what I can say of you I have no doubt he will allow you to refer to him. That will be tip-top—nothing better."

"Refer to him!" That was another phase of city experience.

"Do you mean that I am obliged to refer to somebody who knows me in order to get a place?"

"Certainly."

"For what?"

"For your character, to be sure," said Carter,

laughing. "Nothing is taken for granted here, unless it is that every man is to be considered a rogue till he proves himself to be otherwise."

"But how can anybody take me for a rogue when they know nothing of me."

"That is just the difficulty," returned Carter. "When nothing is known of you, you are taken at the worst possible valuation. Don't you see that is the only safe business rule?"

"No, I don't; with us in the country it is just the other way."

"It won't do here, though," said my friend; "you will soon understand why."

"New York must be a pretty hard place."

"Well, it is and it isn't. There are all sorts and sizes jumbled together. I call it a good place. If a man is honest and industrious, and sticks to his business, he is very sure to get along. So don't be discouraged (Carter could not fail to observe that I looked chagrined), it may be weeks before you get any thing to suit you. Keep trying; the right thing will turn up after awhile, and then you will go ahead — no mistake about it."

I felt thankful to Carter for his attempt to cheer me, for I confess my courage was not quite at the point I could desire. I assented to his prediction, and bidding him good night I climbed manfully upward till I reached the attic, and quite overcome by the day's excitements soon fell asleep.

CHAPTER VII.

THE next day, according to promise, Carter introduced me to Mr. Embury, the senior partner of the firm he was with, and with whom I perceived he had been conversing.

I was received very kindly. "Glad to see you, Mr. Powers. You are just from the country, I learn. We want good industrious young men like yourself here. Mr. Carter has been speaking to me about you. It is all right. Send them to me. I will take care of them."

I felt much like prolonging an interview began so agreeably, but a look from Carter, who stood by, warned me to take leave of the busy merchant. I thanked him, therefore, and came away.

I will not recount the wearying details of my attempt to procure a good position in this large and confusing city. I labored at the work with unceasing energy, but it appeared as if the "heavens were biass" against me. I answered every advertisement that looked at all like what I wanted. I ventured to spend a few dollars in advertising, myself. I took a list of the first-class houses and went the rounds of all of them. Nobody wanted to employ me on any terms I could afford to engage for.

It was curious to witness the different manner with which I was received at different places. Some would treat me with kind civility while they returned a courteous negative to my application; others would jerk out a gruff "No," or give a surly shake of the head, without deigning to favor me with a look. Occasionally I was made the butt of a poor jest, which, however, affected me but little. It was the kind response, accompanied by a refusal, which discouraged me more than any other reception.

I have always felt very grateful to Carter for endeavoring to keep me in spirits.

"Don't give it up," he would say. "You will strike the right spot by and by. I was quite as long myself before I could get a place, and you see I have never left it."

.   .   .   .   .   .

I had spent my last dollar, for I paid my board weekly, and had borrowed a few shillings of Carter to help me to an omnibus ride when too much fatigued walking.

Notwithstanding my want of success, the longer I staid in New York the less discouraged I felt. For during the six weeks of my peregrinations over the city I had pretty nearly got rid of my green look, indeed of my greenness generally. That was only superficial. I soon discovered it was not difficult to acquire the ready habit and quick apprehension of city life, that also was superficial.

My six weeks' experience was very valuable to me. I learned much that I could not have gained in any other way; and got an insight into the character of some first-class men, when

they were off their guard and had no object in
disguising it.

.   .   .   .   .   .

One afternoon I took the horse-car of the
Sixth Avenue Railroad to ride up town, for I had
walked a great deal that day and was tired out.
Before reaching Canal Street we met with an
obstruction in the shape of a truck which had
broken down while crossing the track. This
detained us perhaps fifteen minutes.

While seated there a gentleman who sat next
me, on my right addressed some casual remark
to me. I replied, and he continued the conversation.

At length my companion exclaimed rather abruptly: "Have you succeeded in finding a place
yet?"

In my amazement I turned and looked the
speaker full in the face.

He was a man I should say about fifty, with
fine expressive features, and dark searching eyes,
which were turned not unpleasantly on me.

3*

"You were in my store the other morning," he continued, seeing that I did not answer. "You may have forgotten it."

"I have been in so many it is impossible to remember all."

"Do you not recollect," said he; "I asked you where you were from."

"I do now recollect it."

"And have you succeeded?"

"No."

"I was so much occupied I could not attend to you. I meant to tell you to come in the next day, but my attention was called away at that moment. You quitted me very abruptly."

I made no reply.

"So you are from New Hampshire?" continued the gentleman.

"Yes."

"What part?"

"From the upper Valley of the Connecticut."

"What county?"

"Grafton."

"Why, I am from Grafton County myself," said the gentleman, smiling.

"You from Grafton County," I exclaimed, in astonishment.

"Why not?" he said, good-naturedly, "and if you will look in on me to-morrow morning at nine o'clock, I will see what can be done for you."

"Where," I asked, still much surprised.

The stranger took a pencil from his pocket, and writing on the margin of a newspaper in his hand, he tore off the slip and handed it to me.

"It is the corner where I got in," he said hastily, as the car stopped at Twenty-third Street, where he left it and walked rapidly toward the Fifth Avenue.

I watched his retreating form as long as I could, and then examined the scrap of paper. The writing was not very legible, but I had no difficulty in making out the words, "Gardner, Lynde & Co.," which I at once recognized as one of the largest commercial houses in the city.

My heart beat quick with excitement. Was this one of the firm? And which one? What would be the result of to-morrow's interview?

"I will not be too sanguine," I said to myself; "it may amount to nothing, after all."

I told Carter about it in the evening.

"You don't say so," he exclaimed. "It was Gardner himself. I know, by your description. He begun a poor boy. I told you that you would hit it after awhile."

"But I don't know yet, whether I have hit it or not," I replied.

"You may count it for certain," said Carter. "He wouldn't take all this trouble for nothing, you may rely on that," and the conversation closed.

Punctually at nine, I was at the counting-room of Gardner, Lynde & Co. I inquired for Mr. Gardner, and had the wit to·say I called by appointment.

After a little delay I was ushered into his private apartment. He was engaged reading his letters, but he signed to me to be seated.

When he had finished he turned and addressed me, but with none of the familiarity of the previous day. His demeanor was serious and in a sense reserved, but his tone was that of kindness.

In the interview, which lasted possibly fifteen minutes, he put to me almost every conceivable question about myself, all of which I answered promptly, though I confess I did not see the necessity of so strict an examination, for it not only embraced every particular of my life in the country (with the exception of my love affair), but every petty circumstance relating to my sojourn in New York.

" You say," concluded Mr. Gardner, " that you understand book-keeping."

" I do."

" Please let me see your handwriting; you may copy a couple of lines there."

I complied, nothing loath to exhibit my penmanship.

"You may remain," said Mr. Gardner, after glancing at the paper. "It is best for you to lose no more time."

He rose and left the room returning in three or four minutes.

"Come with me," he said. "This gentleman will set you at work," he continued, introducing me to one of the head men. "After a few weeks we can tell where to place you."

The work I was set at was to aid in loading some boxes of merchandise; not exactly what I anticipated, but I went at it with hearty good-will, astonishing even the carmen with the display of my strength and dexterity. After so long a period of suspense and anxiety it was a luxury to be permitted to earn a living even by helping to load a cart.   .

I returned to my boarding-house at night in a state of healthful fatigue. Carter was perfectly delighted.

"You are all right now," he said. "Keep doing, no matter what you are put at, if it is driving an old dray-horse. Gardner wants to find out what you are made of."

I continued industriously at the same sort of work for a week, and was then advanced a little, that is, I was employed in a higher kind of service, which was relieved occasionally by being sent on various commercial errands.

Every week I earned six dollars, which barely enabled me to live. But I was content, more than content, I was happy. I had secured a place in one of the first establishments in the city, and knew it depended on myself to retain it and be advanced in it. It was with intense satisfaction I could inform my parents of the good news. Hitherto my letters must have proved meager and unsatisfactory.

CHAPTER VIII.

I REMAINED with the house of Gardner, Lynde & Co. nearly three years and a half.

I look on this period of my life with much satisfaction. From the day I entered the place till I left, I devoted myself with unwavering and steady energy to my duties. I commenced with zeal by assisting to load' the drays. Mr. Gardner, though appearing not to notice me, really watched me closely.

At the end of six months I was promoted to the counting-room, and my salary doubled. I never asked for any change of position or increase of wages, but worked hard and faithfully. It was now, that my excellent education at the Academy produced its fruits. I could not help perceiving in this respect that I was far superior to the other young men in the store, and as to mere details the knowledge of these was easily acquired.

It was the autumn of 1857 when I came to New York. In the autumn of 1860 I was at the head of my department, which was the most important in the establishment.

In this position I saw much of Mr. Gardner, who conferred with me daily. Indeed he had on more than one occasion hinted that at the end of five years from the commencement of my service, he should give me an interest as one of the junior partners.

Of this period of five years, over three had expired. I can not express the emotions of pride and gratification with which I informed my parents of the brilliant prospect which was before me, and which I felt I had gained by my faithful assiduity. Thus far there had not been a check to what seemed to me a triumphant progress. All my thoughts and efforts had been directed to the business, nothing but the business, of my employers. I attended church on

Sunday it is true, but I fear my thoughts were mainly in the counting-room. As to female society, I had solemnly resolved to have none of it. My experience with Emma Parks had cured me for all time, as I then felt, of any desire to cultivate it. I had a bowing acquaintance with several young ladies of the congregation, but nothing further. I had been invited occasionally to parties, but I declined with a feeling of grim resistance.

I was often bantered on what was termed my aversion to the sex, indeed, my kind New England landlady took frequent occasions to say it was not a good sign when a young man neglected the society of virtuous young ladies, and she cautioned me against falling into the habit. If such were my tastes now, what would I get to be when I grew older. Others would declare I had been crossed in love, and hoped I would get over it some time. I stoutly withstood all these insinuations, suggestions, banterings, and jesting, keeping on my way undisturbed.

Every summer I visited home, and rejoiced my parents with the improvement in my appearance, and the account of my prospects. There I would hear Mrs. Emory often spoken of, but the charm had dissolved. The name no longer sent the blood bounding quickly through every vein. My tastes began to partake of the refinements of metropolitan life. The girls of my native place did not look as handsome or as well-dressed, or as "fine," as they used to do.

I was now the observed of all observers in the village church. I was always particular in my dress; and after I was firmly established in my situation, I could afford to indulge myself in this respect. Without vanity, I may say my personal appearance was good, so that with the aid of a first-class New York tailor, I could not fail to attract the attention of my country friends and acquaintances, with whom I began to pass for a "great New York merchant."

In going to and returning from my native town, I went by different routes, making a wider circuit, in order to see some of our noted places for summer resort. In this way I visited Saratoga, and Lake George, and Niagara, and even went once to Montreal. I was at the same time at great pains to improve my manners, and to acquire general information, but my heart was in the counting-room, my sole purpose was to get rich.

It is with reluctance I take leave of this part of my life, I was so happy and contented in it.

CHAPTER IX.

WHAT American can forget the gloom of the winter preceding the breaking out of the rebellion. This gloom began to cast its shadow immediately after the November elections, and spread deeper and deeper over the land till the actual commencement of hostilities, when it was dissipated by the swift and stirring events of the war. It settled over the merchant, the artisan, the mechanic, the laborer. Above all, it gathered thick about the heart of every one who cherished the grand hope of an undivided nationality for our common country.

I could lay no claim to belong to this last class, for my soul was too deeply engrossed in trade to be stirred by the possibilities of the hour. I lamented over a dull fall business, and thought of but little else.

.   .   .   .   .   .

I was seated alone with Mr. Gardner in his private room one afternoon, the latter part of December, engaged in making a special report on the condition of the debts due to the firm, from each of the Southern States, preparatory to the usual balance-sheet for the first of January.

I perceived Mr. Gardner exhibited none of his usual elasticity of spirits. He was very serious, while a resolute, I may say dogged expression overspread his face.

As I concluded, he asked, "What is the sum total of the indebtedness?"

"Do you mean that which I have marked undoubted?" I said.

"I mean the whole. You will find there will be no difference in them," replied Mr. Gardner, setting his teeth firmly together.

I went over the abstract, adding the various amounts together, and shortly replied, "Nearly three millions."

"About as I thought," said Mr. Gardner.

He half opened his lips, as if to go on, then he said, abruptly, "That will do," and I left him.

For myself, I had not thus far entertained the slightest apprehension that there *could* be a war, although South Carolina had already "seceded." I looked on it as a large game of brag by the politicians on both sides. I was so engaged in my daily work, that I had almost ceased to have but the one thought—how to thrive in it. It may be humiliating to confess this, but I was one of a great class, who care little for any interests except what affects their personal avocations.

Going home I revolved in my mind the words and manner of my principal. He was evidently alarmed at the aspect of things. But even then, I could not bring myself to consider it to be serious.

I was soon to be undeceived.

The month of January satisfied the most hopeful merchant, that the worst was coming;

if not in our national, at least in our commercial affairs. I did not realize this; for I was
inexperienced in reverses; but our firm did.

I never shall forget my sensations when Mr.
Gardner said to me in a quiet calm tone:

"Powers, you will soon witness a great crisis. All houses who have dealt with the South
largely must break."

I did not then think he included his own
firm. He saw I did not, and continued, "You
do not suppose we can lose three millions and
go on, do you?"

The clerks and employees of a large successful mercantile house, regard their principal as
soldiers do a favorite general: they not only feel
safe with him, but no idea of disaster enters their
minds while he commands.

When Mr. Gardner asked me this question,
it astounded me more than if he had struck
me a blow in my face. The house of Gardner,
Lynde & Co. not go on! *They* stop! This
magnificent edifice, with all its appurtenances

and appliances, be closed! All the ramifications of this enormous business suspended!

My head swam. I think I must have been seized with faintness, for a moment after I found myself seated in a large arm-chair.

Mr. Gardner regarded me with a compassionate look. "My young friend," he said, "you have but yet learned your A B C in affairs. Doubtless you consider yourself a competent, well-trained merchant, and so you are; but I repeat, it is only the A B C of commercial life that you have studied, which is the prosperous, successful, sunny side. You can never be a full-grown man till you have experienced the reverse of this. If you are wise, the lesson you will soon learn will last you a lifetime. Try to make the most of it."

"But," I interposed, "when this comes from no fault, mistake, or negligence of your own, it is very aggravating."

"On the contrary, that is why there is nothing aggravating about it," said Mr. Gardner,

4

"and as to the cause," continued he, "I would rather be ruined fifty times over, and become literally a beggar than that our country should be scattered into fragments, and hold no longer a place as a great nation."

Mr. Gardner continued the conversation much in the same strain. He saw how deeply I was affected by what threatened him (for, truly, in this I had lost sight of the utter demolition of my own prospects), and he strove to impress on me a serviceable lesson.

I returned home that evening prostrated in body and mind, with loss of courage, resolution, and energy. I did not dare speak with Carter, for I could not betray private confidential remarks, so I had to suffer in silence.

I went from that time to my daily labors, now labors indeed, with lead at my heart and a millstone around my neck, working painfully on through the winter, through the spring to April, through April to the 12th of that month, when the first gun against Sumter settled the fate of our commercial house and changed forever the destiny of the country.

Long before this my feelings had been roused to the highest pitch of excitement. Mr. Gardner himself was full of zeal and activity, so were all in the establishment. There was very little to attend to during the day, and in the evening the young men were busy drilling, while the more advanced among them were already waiting for marching orders.

The older men were attending meetings of committees, devising plans to raise money to aid recruiting, and arranging for places in which to receive the soldiers. In short, doing every thing possible to aid and strengthen the government.

The house of Gardner, Lynde & Co. suspended: but what was that to the STOP threatened the nation!

All was excitement, confusion, rapid preparation. The streets so recently filled with persons and vehicles employed only in peaceful pursuits, were resonant with the rattling of artillery wagons, and the tramp of armed men, whose bright polished guns and bayonets glittered in the sunlight—a strange, solemn spectacle.

The parks were converted into barracks; additional hospital accommodations were got ready, and all the energies of the people directed to preparing for war.

My resolution was taken. I wrote to my parents that I intended to enlist. My father, my thoughtful quiet father, returned immediate answer that he well knew what my decision would be before receiving my letter. He gave me many brave words of encouragement, and exhorted me to do my duty manfully. My mother added a trembling signature to my father's letter.

I was soon at the head of a company of young men. I obtained a captain's commission without delay, and my regiment shortly after received orders to proceed to Washington.

The story of the war is familiar to us all. Its history has been published in multifarious .

ways and forms. I do not propose to add a single chapter to it.

During the summer campaign in Virginia my company were on one occasion deployed as skirmishers. While thus engaged, I was fired on from an ambush and received three bullets, one of which shattered my arm below the elbow, another inflicted a severe flesh wound in my thigh; the third just missed my left lung.

I dropped senseless and, as I was doubtless supposed to be dead, escaped being made prisoner. Later in the day the ground was occupied by our own troops, and I was borne off in a very exhausted and apparently dying state. But my hardy constitution, together with the excellent care I received in the hospital, saved my life, which, for some time, was in imminent danger.

My wounds proved so serious that the surgeon was of opinion I could not again enter the service, and accordingly I received from the war department an honorable discharge.

In the month of October I had sufficiently

recovered to be able to bear the journey home.
How lovely looked my native hills! The air, so
pure and elastic, seemed to breathe fresh life in
me. As we drove to the door my father and
mother, who were anxiously expecting me, stood
ready to lift me out, and I was soon reclining
in my own little chamber, surrounded by every
comfort, and cheered by the attentions of the
entire neighborhood.

My convalescence was rapid. I could take
exercise, and with exercise came a renewal of
force and vigor. I was quite the lion of the
country round, as the first returned soldier of
the war. I had come home severely wounded,
and I was honored for what I had endured.

CHAPTER X.

By the following spring I had regained my natural health and strength. During the long New Hampshire winter, I thought a great deal of what I was now to do. This had indeed become a serious question.

As the spring opened I could no longer restrain myself. I must return to New York, though I had heard that every department of business was stagnant. As the phrase is, nothing was doing.

Not daunted, however, I started once more for the metropolis. It had the appearance of an armed camp. I sought my old boarding-house. It was not occupied. Carter I knew was in the war. So were nearly all my fellow-clerks. Mr. Gardner had gone to Europe in order to effect, if possible, some arrangement with his

creditors, nearly all of whom resided abroad, so
that he might resume business. Not one of the
old firm was in the city.

I selected a respectable boarding-house, and
took possession of a pleasant room assigned to
me, for there was no lack now of empty apartments, and at very moderate prices. On Sunday
I was greeted by many old acquaintances, who
seemed glad to see me, and who expressed the
hope that I had quite recovered. I saw, however, that there was not the slightest danger of
my being made a hero because I had been
wounded. The city was full of just such heroes,
their arms in slings, or on crutches, or sauntering along pale and sickly-looking from loss of
blood.

When I left the service of Gardner, Lynde
& Co. I had saved up about seventeen hundred
dollars. My personal expenses preparing for
the campaign were large. While stretched for
dead on the field, I was despoiled of my watch
and boots, and fifty dollars which were on my

person. My disbursements afterward further reduced my store, so that on arriving in New York I had scarcely two hundred dollars remaining.

I spent several days looking about to mark the changes which had taken place, and to endeavor to get the run of affairs. Things were at a very discouraging ebb. Every species of property, real and personal, was selling at ruinously low prices. Gold had not yet advanced beyond five or six per cent., and dullness characterized the Stock Exchange.

Passing one morning through Wall Street, I felt a hand placed familiarly on my shoulder, and heard a voice, which was not familiar, exclaim, "How are you?"

I turned, and recognized the speaker as a person who used frequently to come to our place to introduce customers, or to offer an invoice of goods, from which a small commission was earned.

With this man I had comparatively but a

slight acquaintance. I had never been prepos-
sessed in his favor.

His history I knew very well. His name
was Horace Deams. He had the appearance of
a person of forty-five, though I dare say he was
considerably older. For prior to 1836 he had
figured as partner in one of the largest silk
houses in the city. Going down in the crash
of 1837, he afterward successfully established
himself as a wholesale grocer. Failing again
in 1847, he recuperated once more, only to go
down beyond hope of resuscitation in the financial maelstrom of 1857. After that, he maintained
himself by introducing several of his old customers to other houses, and acting as broker in
various ways, in stocks, in merchandise, and in
real estate; sometimes, in more questionable
schemes.

This man was of an imposing, portly figure,
and always dressed, not only handsomely, but with
faultless taste. His face struck you, on first introduction, as rather agreeable than otherwise. It

was not till you became better acquainted with him that you looked on it with aversion or disgust.

Mr. Horace Deams maintained a suave, unctuous pretension, differing entirely from the bold, egregious assumption of some men. He had so much business on his hands! He must see an "important party" at two, and it lacked but five minutes of that hour. Another "party" had to be met at three, and no time was to be lost. Still another "party" would dine with him, that very day, when a large "operation" was to be entered into.

It was, nevertheless, always easy to induce Mr. Deams to disregard these set hours, if any hope of a "transaction" could be held out, so that the young fellows about the establishment began at last to suspect that, in fact, he had not so very much to attend to after all.

In my position, as one of the head men, Mr. Deams was by no means to my taste. I think he saw it, but it made no difference in his bland, oily dignity.

This was the individual that placed his hand on my shoulder, saying, " How arc you ?"

I never used to relish encountering Deams on any occasion. Now, the sight of him afforded me a species of pleasure. It reminded me of the time when we were in the full tide of business and every thing was moving prosperously. This man was associated in my mind with that period, and I returned his greeting with something of cordiality, not permitting myself to be unpleasantly affected by his patronizing air.

After the first salutations, Deams exclaimed:—

" So you have got enough of fighting ?"

" No, I have not," I retorted ; " but I have been laid up for nine months, and do not expect to go back to the service at present."

" Wise determination, young man," continued Deams, " very wise. Let the politicians fight it out, I say. They began it."

" Mr. Deams, if you have no better opinions to express, I must wish you good morning."

" Not so fast, not so fast, Mr. Powers," returned Deams, composedly. "Every one to his opinion, and you are welcome to yours. I wanted particularly to see you; very particularly."

"Indeed?"

"Yes. I have some business matters I want you to take hold of with me. Here is my office; step in just for one moment (he saw I hesitated), to see where I am."

Mr. Deams led the way into a small basement room, in which was his desk and one or two chairs.

"Good enough for such times as these," he observed, carelessly. "No rent to pay, you understand. The landlord was only too glad to have me occupy it; much better for him than to leave it vacant, which is the situation of half the offices on the Street. But things are on the turn, mark me, I say, things are on the turn. I have been here the whole time watching for it."

I might have remarked before that Deams was a man of quick observation, by no means deficient in intellect, and with his long and varied experi-

ence, not a bad judge of affairs generally. His
last remark struck me, but I made no reply.

"I want you to dine with me to-day, at five
o'clock," he continued—"sharp five," and Mr.
Deams placed a card in my hand, with his name
and address handsomely engraved on it.

I hesitated a moment, and then said, "I will
come."

CHAPTER XI.

It is an old proverb, that misery makes one acquainted with strange bedfellows.

I would never have believed it, had it been said of me twelve months before, that I should, on such a day, be dining with Horace Deams as his guest.

I felt myself *above* this man; first, as connected with one of the strongest commercial houses in the city; again, from a satisfied sense of personal mercantile integrity. For recollect, reader, there is Pharisaism in affairs, marked and conspicuous; quite as marked and conspicuous as in religion.

While walking along that afternoon, on my way to the residence of Deams, which I was rather surprised to find, by inspection of his card, to be in a fashionable quarter, I asked myself, what was my object in accepting his invitation. Honesty compelled me to answer that it was because I hoped to derive some personal advantage from the visit. The idea humiliated me, but it was a fact, nevertheless. Things had so changed, that I was hoping for something to come of an interview with a man I had despised, and, I may say, *did* despise.

I was learning my first lesson.

On finding the number indicated, I perceived it to be a first-class boarding-house, and on inquiring for Mr. Deams, at the door, I was received by the man-servant with a great show of deference, and ushered to a handsome parlor on the second floor, where a table was elegantly laid with covers for two. A wine-cooler stood near, with champagne.

Presently Deams entered from a side door, which I perceived led to his sleeping-room.

He received me with easy politeness, in which was mingled a kind of pomposity, not altogether unbecoming his large, obese form.

"I am glad to find you are punctual," he observed. "Punctuality in all things, especially in appointments, more especially in a dinner appointment is one of the virtues."

He rang the bell. "John, serve dinner."

This order given, Mr. Deams proceeded. "Yes, punctuality is my motto; without it, I could never get through the numerous operations which crowd upon me—never."

"I thought things were very dull at present?" I remarked.

"Oh, I don't speak of the moment, I refer, generally, to what I have to do; and the man does not exist who can say Horace Deams ever failed to meet an appointment. But here is dinner."

We sat down, and the conversation, for a time, was nearly suspended. It was evident Mr. Deams had the tastes of an epicure, and was not willing to interrupt his gastronomic delights by any attempt at discoursing, of which he was usually so fond.

As his appetite gradually became less demanding, he began to season the repast with various observations, oracularly delivered, until—the dessert and wine only remaining to be dealt with—he settled into a species of homily on the morals of trade.

I felt instinctively that the old fellow was endeavoring to corrupt me. In other words, he was trying to alter my standard of honesty.

"Wait," said he, "till you have had my experience, and you will see things as they are. My family, as you know, are of the highest respectability. I inherited a handsome sum from my father, who brought me up closely to business; and, take my word for it, there was not a more competent or more active young man in the city. I was established early, on my own account, as partner in one of the leading houses—just as good a house, my young friend, as that of Gardner, Lynde & Co. before *they* failed."

I could not help wincing at the term "failed,"

applied to such a castle of commercial strength as was our firm.

"You will get used to such things in time," continued Mr. Deams, seeing that I changed color. "Your people were but men, and their means, like those of every merchant, 'in supposition,' as Shakespeare says, and 'there be land-rats, and water-rats' always attempting to gnaw a hole into them. No man can call himself safe, Mr. Powers, no man."

I gave an assent to this general proposition.

"To go back to myself," continued Mr. Deams. "The house in which I was a partner suspended; went all to flinders—Why? ¬Not because we had not sufficient capital in the concern, for we had: but because people owed us more than the amount of that capital, and wouldn't or couldn't pay. I tried this three times," said Deams with a melancholy tone, after draining his glass of champagne and refilling it, "three times I tried it, and then—'out.' Now I want you to profit by my experience."

"It seems to me at that rate I should not go into business at all," I replied.

"I don't say you would not be right. For it is a mere lottery, with nearly all blanks. Look at it, you spend your life slaving to support knaves, who cheat you out of your money and your earnings."

"Not quite so bad as that I hope."

"Yes it is. There is no real honesty, and not a particle of honor, in the whole ramification of affairs."

"I can not hear you say that without contradiction," I retorted, with some warmth; "I myself know to the contrary. I am acquainted with many individuals who are governed in their dealings by the most scrupulous ideas of honor and honesty."

"All conventional, sir," returned Deams, waving his hand, as if brushing my remarks aside, "nothing but conventional. I tell you mere conventional morality, is the morality of trade. I know what you are going to say," he continued,

"I know all the sacrifices the merchant is ready to make to meet his engagements, how he strains every nerve to sustain his credit. Again I ask you, why? Because *not* to meet those engagements ruins him, and to allow his credit to suffer, is to commit suicide. So, keeping up one's credit is keeping up one's self. It is all selfishness, nothing but selfishness—looking out for number one. Nothing high-minded or honorable about it. Talleyrand gave the correct definition of 'business,' when he declared it to be ' *L'argent d'autres* '—other folk's money; ha, ha, ha; other folk's money."

The working in of this little scrap of French appeared to soothe Mr. Deams's feelings, for he continued in a much less excited manner.

As I saw it was useless to discuss the subject with him, I endeavored to gradually draw him from it. This was not easy. He evidently was determined to finish his discourse. At the same time, he mixed so much shrewd sense with his observations and his arguments to prove the morals of trade were any thing but good morals, showed so much insight in the motives of a large class, that I confess I listened with interest, while I shook my head at his conclusions.

Dinner was at length over. Deams lighted his cigar, after offering me one, and wheeling his chair round into a friendly relation with mine, he commenced: "Now, Mr. Powers, for what I want to say to you. This present state of stagnation is over: things begin to work. We are getting on a war basis. We shall have the largest sort of operations on foot growing out of it. You are just the one to take advantage of this, and I am just the one to pilot you. Speculation will begin this very summer. The Government are getting ready their paper money, and it will put every thing under full headway by Fall. Another year and things will be rampant."

"What prevents your taking advantage of it?" I asked.

"'Horace Deams'—I mean the name—is played

out, my friend, played out. I am making an honest confession. It no longer goes current. I can not conjure with it as I used to. I know how to originate, how to plan, and advise, but I must have a fresh man to execute, you see. The speculative world likes things with new faces, and new men to operate them, and we must humor it."

I did not manifest the least enthusiasm at the announcement of Mr. Deams's proposition. On the contrary I maintained an ominous silence.

" You certainly do not misunderstand me, when speaking of myself," he exclaimed, in a tone of some alarm. " No one sustains a better social position in this city than I. No one has a higher reputation as a man of honor. But old enterprises have passed away and old ideas. This is a new era; an era of new men; an era, I may say, of young men. I hope, Mr. Powers, you do not misunderstand me?"

"Oh, no. I do not think, however, I shall

prove a good hand at what you call speculation."

"The very best in the world, sir, take my
word for it."

"What makes you think so."

"Well," replied Deams, hesitating in the most
natural manner, "I really do not want to flatter
you, Mr. Powers, but you have what I call a first-
class address."

"I hope you mean an honest address," said I,
unable to keep from laughing.

"That is just what I do mean," said Deams,
seriously.

"And you do not expect me, I hope, to
do any thing dishonest under cover of this address?"

"Oh, no, no, no," exclaimed Deams in a deprecatory tone, coloring at the same time. "How
oddly you take matters."

"Not at all. I wished merely to arrive at
your exact meaning."

"It is this, Mr. Powers. Your business connections are good. You yourself fresh, active, and persevering. A proper enterprise in your hands—mark you, I say, a good, honest enterprise in your hands, with me for an adviser, will be sure to succeed. That is just what I mean."

We continued the conversation, much in this way, late into the evening. In conclusion, Mr. Deams was very anxious I should make his office my head-quarters. He said that I had better spend the early part of the season in accustoming myself to the ways of the Street, which were not to be learned in a counting-room; and that, although things were dull, I could, no doubt, do something as stock-broker, "which is always," said Mr. Deams, soothingly, "respectable—highly respectable—quite different from your poor devil of a note-broker."

At length I bade my new friend good-night, without committing myself to any of his propositions, but gave a partial promise to call on him the next day.

5

As I walked home that evening I felt a
sense of *diminution* such as I never before experienced. It was in consequence of my com-
panionship with a man who endeavored to
weaken my faith in human nature; a man whose
judgment of others was formed by always at-
tributing to them selfish motives.

Still were not his judgments in the main correct? Perhaps so, but the *rationale* was a low
one.

I resolved not to go near Mr. Deams's office,
but endeavor to secure something to do in a
mercantile establishment.

I found my situation very different from
what it was when I first entered New York.
Then, as a youth almost, I could lay my hand
to any thing; could take up with any thing that
would honestly procure me a living. Now, as
an educated merchant, after occupying the position I had done with Gardner, Lynde & Co., it
was scarcely consistent with my self-respect to
begin my career again as assistant porter or

errand boy, even if I could get such a place, which a lad of nineteen could much better fill.

I made many inquiries, and found to my mortification that Deams had not exaggerated the stagnation in trade.

I was greatly discouraged and out of spirits. The small amount of money I had would not last long. What was to be done!

While in this state I again encountered this man. He was excessively cordial. He made no allusion to my not calling on him; he only asked if I had been out of town, and said he had just received a small commission to execute for the purchase of some merchandise, which he would give to me, as it was quite in my line. He told me what it was, and I proceeded with him to his office to get the particulars, and was delighted to find the matter to be as Deams had stated.

I started at once to fill the order, which my knowledge and experience enabled me to do in a very satisfactory manner. The commission earned was not large, but it was promptly paid. Deams indignantly refused to share it with me. He was only happy to throw something in my way. He was sure I would do the same by him if opportunity presented.

.   .   .   :   .   .   .

CHAPTER XII.

I will not weary the reader with the details of the two or three succeeding months. Indeed, I can not myself bear to recall them.

By degrees I became more habituated to the society of Deams. His flow of spirits was constant. The future was to him a vast treasure-house. He would make my fortune and his own long before another twelvemonth passed. Meantime, if I cared to trouble myself with insignificant commissions, he could throw plenty of them in my way. In fact, he sometimes did so.

In spite of my mental resistance, the man began to take the position of benefactor. It is true, I had no respect for him, and he must have known it, but alas! I began to have less and less respect for myself.

I used to wonder how Deams got the money to live as he did, and at length I asked him the question.

He laughed, and said, "Do you remember Burke's famous apostrophe to the credit system?"

"No."

"You should read it. I can only say it meets my entire approval."

"Do you mean that you get your apartments without paying for them?"

"I *shall* pay, of course," said Deams, "but not till we launch one of the many great enterprises I have on foot. I confess I owe my landlady a pretty good sum. So much the better. She has made the investment, and it won't do for her to ask me to quit, lest she should lose it. I keep the bait always before her and stay on."

"Shameful," I exclaimed,—"perfectly shameful!"

"How so?" said Deams. "Don't I tell you I *intend* to pay her? And I shall add a handsome *douceur* for her forbearance, but she must wait—she must wait."

.   .   .   .

When I left Gardner, Lynde & Co., I thought I knew New York and its business, and the ways of doing business; but after being awhile in Wall Street I was obliged to confess myself a novice.

I met a good many people whom I knew, and occasionally was enabled to do something in a legitimate way. Sometimes I was made a dupe of, but not twice, I think, in the same way.

Once an old fellow by the name of Eli Nichols, who had an office in which he used to "shave" notes and attend to various transactions, gave me an order to purchase some land warrants for him at a certain price.

I went industriously about, inquiring for them at all the leading brokers, but could find none, though the nominal quotation was two or three per cent. below my limits. I reported to Nichols my want of success.

He thanked me for the trouble I had taken, and said I need do no more about it. I afterward learned that, at that time, he was the principal holder of land warrants, and close on my inquiries, had sent an outside "party" to every place where there was the least probability of my having called, and offered a limited amount of these very warrants, which were quickly taken, in the expectation of selling to me. The old knave in this way disposed of about five hundred warrants, and cleared at least fifteen hundred dollars by his morning's work.

Shortly after three o'clock there was quite a rush to Nichols's office to sell, but he was "not buying at present."

As the reader will understand, I was entirely innocent. I had only been made a tool of. The affair mortified me exceedingly, but I made no complaint to Nichols. He would only have laughed at me had I done so.

.   .   .   .

Thus the weeks slipped by, with Deams as my

chief companion. My occupations were petty, yet they required the exercise of a species of craft to manage them. Whenever I allowed myself to think, I was disgusted with them and with myself. But this became more and more seldom. There is a fascination about the uncertain rapid changes of the Street which attracts and chains one there whenever once actually engaged in them: and, like the strange spell of the gambling-table, exercises an inexplicable power.

I was not as yet making enough to pay my expenses. Deams continued to ridicule my industrious habit of trying to do something. "Wait," he said, "till Fall, and you shall make all the money you want—all you want."

It was on a hot Saturday afternoon, early in July, that, after a particularly profitless week, my spirits sank lower than usual. It was in vain Deams endeavored to encourage me. At last he said: "Come, let us run down to Long Branch and spend Sunday, and see the world in pleasure costume."

5*

I assented moodily. We got on board the steamer for Port Monmouth, and in due time were landed there; then, taking the train, we arrived in a few minutes at that famous place of summer resort.

The bracing sea-air, the excitement of the scenery around, the crowded beach, the whirl of handsome carriages along it, the motley groups of bathers, gave a new direction to my thoughts, and for the time I forgot my other self—the wretched inhabitant of the " Street."

By Monday, I had resolved to spend two or three days more at the sea-shore, and let Deams return to town alone.

He assented readily and with entire good-nature, and I was left to my enjoyment. That was indeed great. I did not attempt to make acquaintances—I had no desire to do so—but I quietly mixed in the crowd or took my solitary walk along the shore or my bath in old ocean.

The beach, as most of my readers may know, is a dangerous one for those who venture outside

5*

the prescribed limits. Nearly every year some one, from folly or negligence, goes beyond and perishes.

I was a good swimmer. I had learned in the swift and sometimes treacherous current of the Connecticut. It was with a real zest that I threw myself into the surf and watched the course of the waves and breasted the dreaded "undertow."

Wednesday came before I could realize a day had passed; Wednesday, when I was to return to New York. I resolved on one more grand swim; I should just have time to take it and get ready for the train.

It was a little past eleven. The surf was alive with human beings. What a masquerade! Age and sex would seem to be perfectly disguised in the strange-looking dresses of every possible description, form, and color. A great many of these were fanciful and expensive, and all were grotesque. I suppose the line of bathers extended up and down for nearly two miles—a curious sight. Everybody was in the noisiest spirits; an odd scene, indeed.

I had taken my last plunge, and was slowly
and reluctantly coming in shore, when there was
a kind of lull in the frolic of the merry makers.
A portentous murmur passed along the line,
Soon it took articulate shape.

"There she is!"   "Where?"   "Which way?"
"Good God! it is not possible."   "What is it?"
"What has happened?"   "A lady carried out!"
"Oh! won't somebody help?"   "Can nothing be
done!"   "Where is a boat?"   "Can't some one
get a boat?"

All this, mingled with various cries and ex-
clamations, fell on my ear in the space of an instant.

Asking a person near me, who appeared less
excited than the rest, where the lady had disap-
peared, I took my resolution.   I had previously
gained a pretty accurate knowledge of the sweep
of the undertow which did not run at once sea-
ward but was drawn to the south, in the direction where I was standing, in a deep, powerful
current.

I struck out boldly toward the point I judged she would be carried to. No one not familiar with such scenes can imagine the difficulties I had to encounter. The continuous break of the waves over my head blinded me, and would have immediately strangled any one not accustomed to the water.

. . . .

I could not see. I could only grasp wildly round. I perceived my strength to be failing, and I was losing courage, when a clear voice from the shore sounded over the waters—" *To the right! more to the right!*" This put new life in me. I struck to the right accordingly. "*Not quite so far!*" "*There!*" "*There!*" "*Just before you!*"

Thus far I had seen no sign or trace of the object of my search. Now, as the crest of the last wave broke over me, I perceived on the top of the succeeding one a something, rag or sea-weed, or broken branch; something which, the next moment clutching, I found was a human being.

I had still strength enough to secure my prize, and sufficient appreciation to turn not directly to the shore, but diagonally, so that I should not encounter the whole force of the undertow, and yet gradually work myself toward the beach. I remember little else, except the rush of a flood, a cataract, then a sense of delight, almost ecstatic, and all was still.

CHAPTER XIII.

My next sensations were terrible. I can compare them to nothing, unless to the imagined horrors caused by the wrangling of fiends in possession of one's soul. No hitherto described agonies of death were equal to what I suffered in coming to life.

At last I opened my eyes. I was in a large airy apartment, where every thing appeared pleasant and comfortable. I essayed to speak, but was prevented by the physician. I looked toward a lady who stood watching me with apparent solicitude. She seemed to anticipate what was passing in my mind, for she said, "You have saved one life, you must not endanger your own by any exertion."

I was satisfied. Closing my eyes again, I fell into a profound slumber. I did not awake till evening. I felt quite well, though I was weak. It was evident I was receiving the most careful attention, for no sooner did I stir than a kind-looking woman, who was acting as nurse, offered me a soothing draught, which I drank eagerly. Then she asked how I felt. I was permitted to speak now, and I replied "Perfectly well, and very hungry."

"How is the lady?" I asked.

"She is getting on remarkably, though it would doubtless have killed an older person."

"Is it a child?" I inquired, carelessly.

"Then you do not know who it is you have saved?"

"No."

"Have you no curiosity about it?"

"Not very much."

"I must tell you, though. One of the most beautiful young ladies that ever lived. Ever so rich; and the very top of the fashion. A New Yorker besides. Miss Worth, Miss Mary Worth."

How much further the nurse might have gone in her description I do not know, but the doctor entering cut it short. To his inquiries I replied that I believed I was perfectly well, only suffering from hunger. However, he permitted me to eat but sparingly, with the promise of further liberty the next day.

I closed my eyes to keep the nurse from talking. I wanted to enjoy the pleasure of thinking. " Miss Worth: Miss Mary Worth." I knew very well who she was—as the nurse said, a very rich and fashionable young lady. Her father, Marmaduke Worth, President of the Bank of Mutual Safety, and one of the capitalists of New York. He, with his family, attended the same church I had, myself, selected when first coming to New York. Yes, I knew Miss Worth well by sight, and should have greatly admired her, doubtless, for she was considered the most beautiful girl in a congregation where there were a great number of beauties, had I not steeled my heart like a flint against any such fascination. Besides, I was too proud to think of any rich girl until I myself was rich.

. . . .

I lay in a charming reverie. "O yes, I recollect her perfectly, every feature, how she dresses, the hat she wears, she is rather tall, not too tall, beautiful form, such a complexion. I remember her eyes, too. She half bowed to me once, from long habit, I suppose, seeing me in church. I took no notice of it; rather savage that. And I have saved *her*, that very girl. Had it not been for me, she would now—she is alive and not injured—that lovely—saved— very beautiful " . . . . .

The reverie I have endeavored to jot down ran gradually into dream, ending in sound sleep.

The second day I felt so well that I rose and dressed myself,. and bade good-bye to my nurse and physician. I walked slowly over to the hotel where the Worths were staying, and inquired of the health of Miss Worth. The mother came into the room immediately. I recog-

nized her as the person who had enjoined prudence on me the first day. After seeing her
daughter in safety, she had come to see' that I
was properly cared for. Mr. Worth shortly
entered the room. I will not repeat the extravagant expressions of gratitude which the lady
uttered.

"We owe you every thing, Mr. Powers, in owing
to you our daughter's preservation," said Mrs.
Worth. "To think of that wretched creature,"
she exclaimed, "who first persuaded Mary to venture farther, and then abandoned her to her fate:
the poltroon who was always boasting of what
he could do in the water."

It was embarrassing to be made the recipi-
ent of such a shower of thanks and blessings
as Mrs. Worth poured on me. Mr. Worth stood
by in silence. At length his wife paused, when
he took occasion to express himself in a most
heartfelt manner.

"I can not feel that I am in any way de-
serving such demonstrations," I said. "I did as

any one would have done in my situation. I heard that a lady was carried away by the undertow—I did not know who—and being accustomed to the water, did what was most natural. I beg you not to consider yourselves under any obligation to me personally."

"Just think of that Manning," broke in Mrs. Worth.

"Who is he?" I asked.

"He is the young gentleman," said Mr. Worth calmly, "who accompanied Miss Worth to bathe. He has the reputation of being an excellent swimmer."

"And stood by quietly to see Mary drown," exclaimed Mrs. Worth.

"Let us say no more about it," said her husband. "Our daughter is safe, and if you will call to-morrow she will be able, I hope, to thank you in person."

Despite my resolve against it, I thought of little else except the next day's interview. I did every thing to kill the time till then. It was useless to conceal a certain agitation as I sent my name in, and was ushered into the private parlor.

Miss Worth rose to greet me in an unaffected manner; she had scarcely grasped my hand, however, before she burst into tears. Her mother appeared much alarmed as she made her sit down.

Miss Worth soon recovered her composure, and looking up, she said very naturally, "Excuse me, I could not help it."

I had a very happy interview. After the first few minutes the conversation took a familiar turn and flowed easily.

Miss Worth gave me an account of how she came in so great peril. She was standing, she said, with Mr. Manning who had hold of her hand, and who had assured her there was no danger, when she suddenly felt herself borne off her feet and carried away.

"Were you conscious when I seized you?"

"Yes. From the first I did not attempt to

struggle, and in this way I think I retained my consciousness."

The morning call lasted over an hour—it seemed to me a minute—when I left, promising to repeat my visit the following day.

In this way one day succeeded another, during which my intercourse with Miss Worth became more and more free and unrestricted. She was now well enough to take the usual walks along the beach, in which I was always her companion. Two weeks glided by literally without my being aware of it. I forgot my condition, my surroundings, my very self, in her society. I can not now recollect how I acted or what I said, for it was one prolonged halcyon dream.

I was rudely wakened from it one morning by overhearing a conversation in the corridor into which my room opened. It happened my door was ajar, and I could not shut my ears to what was passing between two young men.

I soon perceived I was the subject of their remarks.

"He will feather his nest, and no mistake," said one.

"That's a fact. It was what I call a lucky swim."

"I wouldn't have taken it, though, for all the girls in New York."

"Perhaps not, but Powers knows the surf like a book."

"They say they are to be married this fall."

"Yes, but the old fellow don't like the idea at all. Would rather give Powers a cool twenty-five thousand, and balance the account in that way. The mother, I am told, goes in for Powers."

"And the girl?"

"Oh, she is all right, of course."

"Shouldn't care about earning a wife that way."

"Nor I. A Newfoundland dog might have done as good service."

"That's a fact."

A sickness came over me. I walked to the window for air.

Swiftly it was all revealed. The old hard
destiny stared me in the face.

I decided at once on my course. The train
would leave in half an hour. I walked to the
hotel where the Worths were staying. It was
too early for a call: so much the better. I
sent my card for Mr. Worth. He came down.
I told him I was there to say good-bye, and
asked him to have the kindness to give my
adieus to his wife and daughter.

Despite his real politeness, I could see an
evident expression of relief overspread his countenance.

"The ladies will be sorry not to see you,
Mr. Powers," he said. "I will communicate your
message. When we return to town we shall
expect to meet you. And,"— here he hesitated,
"if—if I can be of—of any service to you in—
in affairs, may I ask it as a favor, my dear
sir, that you will command me?"

I gulped down an indignant reply, for the
words I heard in the morning were sounding

in my ears, and said as calmly as I could, "Thank you," and thus the interview ended.

In twenty minutes I was driving toward the station. I turned and gave one glance at the room I knew was occupied by Miss Worth. The window was thrown open, and a fair hand waved an adieu from it.

6

CHAPTER XIV.

THE adventure at Long Branch happened just as I was five and twenty. That extra salt-water bath brought about a partial crisis in my destiny. My impression is that just at that time I was fast lapsing into a mere hanger-on of Wall Street ; half reconciled to the idea of living from hand to mouth, and becoming less and less particular as to the method of raising the means.

I did not then have any such opinion of myself, but now looking back to the period, I do it with something like a shudder, for I can see just what I escaped.

The fact is, although, as I have before remarked, I did not sympathize with the views of life entertained and promulgated by Deams, although I could not call him an honest man, even after a tolerably low standard of honesty, yet,

consenting to act with him, at least to co-operate
with him, I was insensibly drifting down to his
standard and falling in with his notions of morality; which, as the reader understands, were of
"The world owes me a living" school; when the
terrible undertow of old ocean gave me a surge
in the opposite direction.

Then was swiftly, suddenly exhibited to me,
just a glimpse of the great BEYOND, and my feelings were still too fresh not to receive a sharp
impression from the PRESENT.

Besides — Mary Worth. No matter what
should come of so peculiar an introduction, even
should nothing come of it, as was most likely, indeed proper, still an event of my life was irrev-
ocably interwoven with an event of the life of a
beautiful young girl; one in whom already I had,
despite myself, taken a romantic interest; an interest such as only young persons can appreciate;
and with whom I was unexpectedly associated in
an occurrence never to be obliterated from her
memory.

The thought of Deams in this connection was absolutely abhorrent to me.

During my journey homeward, I took a new survey of the situation. What does Deams want of me? What does he expect from the connection? After all, am I not to become his dupe when the occasion serves, just as Eli Nichols made a tool of me in the matter of the land-warrants?

Again: was it really to be credited that, as Deams would have me suppose, there was nothing going on in Wall Street but "Pitch and toss," and no rule of the game but "Heads I win, tails you lose," "Hardest fend off," and so forth? Were there not enterprises requiring quick wit, energetic action, firm nerve, and praiseworthy prudence, which should partake neither of trick, humbug, or rascality? Why, then, should I allow a shallow pretender, thrice broken in fortune and of doubtful integrity, to take advantage of my fresh strength and buoyant feelings and uninjured name?

It was with such reflections that I was prepared to enter New York once more.

The recollection of Mary Worth at the window, and of her parting salutation, determined me, and with the strength of a Hercules bracing every nerve, I resolved to renew the contest with other plans· and firmer hopes and more honest appliances. And so I came to the great Babel again.

CHAPTER XV.

READER, I wish I could stop here! You behold me in the full enjoyment of a fresh, unhackneyed and honest resolution. But what says the proverb? "Hell is paved with good intentions." It were a pleasant way to round a story, to depict to you how this sudden change wove a new web for my future, and left nothing for me to do but rise rapidly in the scale under the effect of these new impulses, and of the patronage and assistance of Marmaduke Worth, President of the Bank of Mutual Safety.

I have a pretty long history to recount before I can indulge in any such record, if, indeed, any such is to come. Not that my late resolves were cast aside. Oh, no. I had taken a wrong step by my connection with Deams, and it was not so easy to retrace it.

On reaching town, that individual was the

first to welcome me. I found him at my lodgings, waiting my coming, as he knew I was to arrive that afternoon.

His treatment of me was so flattering, his manner so kind, I may say so deferential, that I lost sight of the unpleasant thoughts I had entertained of him, or if remembered, it was with self-reproach that I could do an unfortunate man so much injustice.

Deams had heard very full accounts of the Long Branch adventure. The journals were filled with it, and my exertions, severe as they really were, had been magnified to grace their columns.

Deams had placed the files, which he had carefully preserved, on my table, and I read, displayed in immense headings, with double leads:

"EXTRAORDINARY OCCURRENCE

AT

LONG BRANCH.

Display of Marvelous Strength, Dexterity.
and Heroism.

A YOUNG LADY SAVED FROM THE JAWS
OF DESTRUCTION. A RESCUE AFTER
BEING SWEPT OUT INTO THE OCEAN.
HENRY POWERS, Esq.,
A Young New Yorker, the Hero.
MISS MARY WORTH, DAUGHTER OF MARMADUKE
WORTH, ESQ., PRESIDENT OF THE BANK OF MU-
TUAL SAFETY, THE YOUNG LADY SAVED."

Following these announcements were "Details
by an Eye-witness"—"Further Details"—"A Correction"—"An additional Correction;" which last
stated "positively and on the very best authority,
that Mr. Algernon Manning did NOT make any
attempt to save Miss Worth, but devoted himself
solely to secure his own safety."

"You see, you see," said Deams triumphantly.
"I always considered you a trump. I saw 'luck'
in your face the first moment I met you, but I
did not think you would throw double sixes so
soon."

Although I could not but be flattered by
what I read, the observation of Deams sounded

coarse and repulsive. When, therefore, he went on to say: "Powers, this affair is worth more to us than a cash deposit to our credit of fifty thousand dollars," my late disgust and suspicion revived.

"How so?" I asked, curtly,

"Why, don't you understand," he replied, with an air of triumph, "that the favor of Marmaduke Worth is the best capital you can have to work on in the Street?"

"Do you think I would take advantage of it?" I exclaimed scornfully.

"Do you mean to say you wouldn't take advantage of it?" retorted Deams, holding his breath.

"That is just what I mean to say, Mr. Deams," was my defiant response.

"Then you are an idiot, and no mistake," was the rejoinder.

I saw the folly of an altercation with Deams, and, on the other hand, he had no disposition to enter on one with me, so after a few words, the

6*

subject was changed, he no doubt believing I
could in time be induced to embrace his suggestions, while I felt sure I should never bring myself to so debasing a situation.

Another matter perhaps insensibly weighed
with me, when I decided it was foolish to fall
out with Deams. I had returned from Long
Branch, after paying my bills, with scarcely five
dollars in my pocket. Going there to spend Sunday, I remained two weeks, and the small sum
which I possessed had melted clean away.

How difficult, from very highest to very lowest, to get rid of an association once formed.

I found myself, in spite of myself, that very
evening in close consultation with Deams about
two or three enterprises, where I could not avoid
perceiving that the most was to be made of the
fact that my name was "free and clear;" which
means, reader, that I had never failed in business, and owed nothing.

"By Jove," said Deams, "I wish I stood in
your shoes, Powers; I mean financially. Wouldn't

I make a fortune, though! Why, a man who owes nothing and has three cents over, can pass for a millionaire."

With all the nonsense Deams was in the habit of uttering, he frequently let drop a sentence which served to set me thinking. This observation was one of that kind. I recorded it in my memorandum book, and it was of use to me on future occasions.

" Well, Mr. Deams, if you could make a fortune were you in my place, you can doubtless instruct me how to make one," I responded pleasantly.

" Of course I can," he replied; " that is what we are together for. I have, as you see, several enterprises on hand. In a few days I shall decide which will draw best, and we will then set to work."

" Meanwhile—"

"Meanwhile what?" interrupted Deams, sharply, as if suspicious that I was about to raise further objections.

"Meanwhile, nothing," I answered, "except that I am out of money."

"Is that all," said Deams. "Don't let that distress you. I will put you all right to-morrow. Depend on me for that."

The next day Deams handed me, for my signature, a beautifully prepared "promissory note," in which the maker, myself, promised to pay to the order of Ezekiel Hubbard, sixty days after date, the sum of five hundred and fifty dollars, value received.

"Sign this," said Deams, "and I will get you the money in fifteen minutes."

"Where?"

"Never you mind where, the money will come, I have already arranged for it."

"Mr. Worth?" I asked suspiciously.

"Don't be such a fool, I beg of you," said Deams, with an injured air. "Mr. Worth, you know, is not in town, and do you think I would attempt such a thing after what you have said?"

"But I don't want five hundred and fifty

dollars. If I must attempt to borrow, fifty is the most I should apply for."

"Which would at once destroy your credit," retorted Deams. "Henry Powers borrowing fifty dollars, indeed! I should like to see him try it as long as I am his friend. The fact is," continued Deams confidentially, "I am a trifle behind myself. I want, say, a couple of hundred dollars; I will stand all the shave. In sixty days people will be back in town, and our company under way; we shall then have all the cash we require for any purpose."

"But why don't you have this note drawn to your order? And who, pray, is Ezekiel Hubbard?"

·"Do you not understand that my name would kill the paper? Every one knows there are lots of judgments against me, and nobody knows any thing *against* Ezekiel Hubbard, I'll be bound," said Deams, laughing.

"But who is he?"

"No matter who he is. I will tell you, though, as a joke. He is the old fellow who saws wood and does odd jobs for me at the house, and he makes a first-rate indorsement, no mistake about it," and Deams laughed again.

I was learning rapidly. The great lesson was, for Wall Street uses, to keep your name so at least nothing can be said against it; and I made another note of that, marking it specially important.

"So you will not tell now where the money is to come from?"

"Yes I will, though," said Deams quickly, "and then you will have the whole story. Eli Nichols will give it to me."

"How much off?"

"Fifty dollars," said Deams stoutly.

"Which you propose to lose?"

"Yes."

"How can you afford it?"

"Why, am I not to have over thirteen thousand dollars early in September from one of the matters we talked over last night?" exclaimed Deams triumphantly; "and do you think I mind

a trifle like this if it serves to give you a lift,
and keep us both easy until then ? "

"Well, for my part," I rejoined, " I don't
like this at all; however, I will think it over
and decide to-morrow."

To-morrow? *There* is the mistake. We hesitate and cry to-morrow, and when it comes,
there is, alas, no improvement over yesterday.
On the contrary, the necessity is stronger; we
see a way out of the immediate distress, and
we accept the present relief, unmindful of what
is to come of it.

Deams practiced the usual trick of his kind;
he undertook to serve my wants and mixed his
own larger ones up with them, thus involving
me to an extent in his necessities while appearing to relieve mine.

It requires a good deal of assurance, certainly,
to profess to be doing one a great and needful
service, when in reality you are actually extorting
a favor instead; but Deams was not lacking in
impudence, and I yielded, almost without know-

ing why, and against my better judgment, to his suggestion.

I thought much about it, however; indeed, that night I slept very little.

"What if I am somewhat behind?" I said to myself, "I have several friends who would not hesitate to lend me a small sum. Why not borrow it? In a few days I can make it good." Then pride interposed, while Deams' subtle argument came to mind, that to borrow a small sum would injure my credit.

In short, it was by a moral weakness such as ninety-nine of a hundred exhibit, that I decided to embrace Deams' offer.

So the note was signed, and Ezekiel Hubbard indorsed it, and the same day Deams gave me, as agreed upon, three hundred dollars. How much he received I never knew, but I dare say Eli Nichols retained a hundred dollars instead of fifty.

Yes, I had the three hundred dollars; but, per contra, time was running away with the sixty days, when five hundred and fifty dollars were to be paid. Would Deams be ready with his portion? I was sufficiently doubtful of the answer to this question to make me careful of the money I received, and except the small sum I had immediate use for, I laid by the whole, determining to practice the strictest economy and make every effort to get something ahead before the note should mature.

As for Deams, he left for Saratoga the day after the affair, and I did not see him again for two or three weeks.

About this time Eli Nichols sent for me to come to his office. I went accordingly. He received me very cordially, and after a few words of a general nature, desired me to make certain brokers an offer for some of the bonds of the Elkton and Buffalo Railroad Company, which were then much depreciated. I saw in the request the repetition of the land-warrant trick, and quietly declined the business.

Eli was much chagrined by my refusal. He

asked what was the matter. "Did I object to earning a commission?"

"Oh no," I replied.

"What then?" said Eli.

"You have never paid me for helping you to make fifteen hundred dollars by the sale of those warrants, and I want you to close that account before we open a new one."

The old fellow flew in a rage. "Young man," said he, "perhaps you desire to quarrel with me. Let me tell you I have driven more than one chap out of the Street who undertook to run against me. I advise you to be getting the money together to pay your note due next month."

"Mr. Nichols," I exclaimed, rising as I spoke, "I have no desire to quarrel with you, but I had as lief do so as not. As to my note, if you will make it an object, I will take it up now. What say you?"

"Time enough when it is due, youngster," retorted the old fellow. "Then you will be down on your marrow-bones for an extension. Don't you think you will get it?"

"Good-day, Mr. Nichols, I perceive you are a little irritated. I will call again some time. Perhaps we can agree on a price for the note," and I left, without having my temper ruffled in the slightest.

This was a real triumph. To show myself independent of the class to which Eli Nichols belonged was a great thing. It taught them I was not to become their serf or bondman, and made me feel stronger by the lesson.

I was exceedingly perplexed, nevertheless, what to do, and I was very glad I had been careful to save my money.

It was now the dullest period of the summer, with really nothing doing. Nearly every one of my acquaintances was away, and even Wall Street appeared deserted. The return of Deams was to me a welcome event, for, with all my resolution, I began to be very desponding. I could see the current of wealth sweep by, and was not able to swim with it or in it. I was only an idle spectator, when I felt that I had the capacity to take part with the strongest.

When with Gardner, Lynde & Co., I had op- portunities of meeting the best business men of the city, and often wondered how such and such a one had risen to wealth and influence on what seemed to me so small a mental capital. I had not yet learned that it is not apt to be the "smart" man, so called, who ultimately suc- ceeds, but rather the careful, industrious, per- sistent person.

I was chafed because there appeared to be no chance for getting a foot-hold, and so I told Deams on our first interview when he was just from the Springs.

"Served you right," he exclaimed: "no busi- ness to be sitting here in the dumps when there was nothing for you to do. Knew it would be just so. You ought to have come with me. I have had a grand time, and am home fresh and fine, and ready to sit down with triple energy to *the* great scheme; for while I have been away I have decided what and when and how! You must take hold in earnest and your fortune is made."

What the "great scheme" was, I will presently explain.

CHAPTER XVI.

I DO not think, in giving this literal history of my life, I should be doing justice to that which I consider the mainspring, did I not speak more particularly of it; since it was now woven into my very being.

Each succeeding day I felt that this influence grew stronger and stronger. So far from trying to resist it, I rejoiced in it and in the abnegation I proposed to myself under it. I *knew* the feeling I entertained toward Mary Worth was in every respect genuine, and honorable to my nature. It helped me to preserve my self-respect when I was tempted to yield to the suggestions of the moment, for I confess I was sustained by no deep well-grounded principle.

The idea of what *she* would think of me, could she know what I was doing, saved me from lapsing into a state of recklessness or indifference, and preserved always within me a strong *ultimate* resolution to become worthy of her—that is, worthy of what I conceived her to be.

I say ultimate resolution, because there are degrees in moral obliquity as well as in moral excellence.

Often when I was engaged in something I could not justify to myself, I would say, "this is unworthy of me." Yet I would go on with the performance.

This was done, however, under a sort of protest of my better self against my worser self; and this is why I use the phrase "ultimate" with reference to what I was, and what it seemed as if I might one day become.

In this connection let me observe that I determined, when the Worth family should return to town, that I would claim no acquaintance with any member of it beyond the ordinary salutation. They should all understand, and especially *she* should understand, I demanded nothing from the accident of having saved her life.

One day, it was early in September, and before the Worths had returned, I met Mr. Worth, who usually came in two or three times a week, face to face on the sidewalk.

He stopped me as I was passing, and gave me his hand very cordially. "I intended to call on you, Mr. Powers, before this," he said, "but when I am in the city I am usually much hurried till I get out of it. In two or three weeks my family will be in town, and I shall then have a better opportunity for seeing you and learning if in any way I can be useful to you."

It was delicately put, and in a manner that could not offend my pride; but I was resolved then and there to define my position apropos of the Long Branch adventure.

"Mr. Worth," I replied, "I am greatly obliged to you for your kindness, but you must permit me to say I have no intention of drawing on it. The nature of the accident which made us acquainted, precludes any possibility of my taking advantage of it to further my interests. I hope Miss Worth has entirely recovered."

"She is quite well," answered Mr. Worth, hurriedly, "quite well, I am thankful to say. Young man," he continued, "I honor you! Good morning."

"I honor you!" The words came spontaneously out of the heart of the old experienced man of Wall Street.

I repeated them several times to myself. "I honor you: I honor you!" What was the capital of fifty thousand dollars which Deams had talked of compared with the reward I had just received? Would I exchange the one for the other? No, indeed.

I entered my office disgusted with its atmosphere and every association connected with it.

Deams was at his desk, in close conference with two or three individuals whose appearance I particularly disliked. He beckoned me to approach, and I was thereupon introduced to Mr. Philo

7

Coldbrook, Mr. Elton Pope, and Mr. Aaron Masterman.

I give these names in full to my readers, because Deams gave them in full to me, and because, further, I have some particular reasons to remember them.

"We were waiting for you, Mr. Powers," said Deams, with a deferential air, which I saw was assumed for some object or other. "These are the gentlemen who control the immense coal-fields I was speaking to you about (it was the first I had heard of them), and Mr. Powers, gentlemen, is the capitalist I told you of."

"Very happy to meet you, Mr. Powers," exclaimed Mr. Aaron Masterman, a portly, big-bellied individual, with small, snuff-colored eyes, rubicund visage, and a delicate pug nose.

"Glad to meet you," he continued, "and talk over matters. We think with your assistance we can make our affair a lively one; if we can coax the market to change—eh?" and Mr. Aaron Masterman laughed a low, coarse laugh, which

added to my disgust, and which caused Deams
to exhibit a frightened air.

"Yes," said Mr. Elton Pope, a small, thin-
visaged fellow, with a yellow wig, very large
protruding orbs, and an immense Roman nose
which occupied nearly his entire face. "Yes,
and we hope Mr. Powers will regard our scheme
favorably."

"We hope so," chimed in Mr. Philo Coldbrook, a tall, spare fellow, with lank hair and
wall eyes which had a sneaking side sweep—"we
hope so."

There was a pause. Even Deams, who usually
was so ready, did not appear to know what to
say.

"Let me have a word with you, Mr. Deams,"
I said at length, proceeding to the front part of
the office.

Deams followed with alacrity. Evidently I
had come in unexpectedly, at least too soon, and
he was as anxious to explain as I was to have an
explanation.

"What does all this mean?" I asked, in a tone of angry impatience.

"Now keep cool, will you," said Deams, soothingly; "keep cool, and don't spoil a fortune for us all by your rashness and irritability."

"Whom do you mean by 'us all?'" I demanded in the same tone.

"Why, you and I, to be sure. But for heaven's sake don't act in this manner! They are watching us."

"Deams," said I, indignantly, "do you expect me to assume any *rôle* you choose to invent for me, without even exhibiting the decency of consulting me on the subject?"

"It is all a mistake, my dear boy, it is all a mistake. I did not know my friends would be in to-day, but when they did come, I could not send them off. I had spoken of you very highly financially, I admit, but in no way which you will disapprove of, I swear to you, when I come to tell you all about it."

"Now *don't* spoil all, *please* don't," he added

beseechingly. " In thirty days our fortune will be made, if you will only hear to reason. This evening you shall look over the papers and judge for yourself. Then accept or reject the scheme, just as you please, only don't be precipitate."

" You don't expect me, then, to give those gentlemen an interview to-day?"

" Certainly not; of course not; indeed, I much prefer you should not," exclaimed Deams hurriedly. " I think you had better just leave us now, and I will explain to——"

" Say what you please, Deams, for yourself, but not a word for me till you have my authority to do so."

" Quite right," interrupted Deams, in his turn, at the same time opening the door of the office, as if fearing the effect of a longer discussion; " quite right, I will be with you early this evening."

What Deams said to his three " friends," I leave the reader to imagine. I only know at the next interview—and there was a next interview—

they seemed doubly impressed with my consequence, and the necessity of conciliating me.

For myself, I left the office in no pleasant
state of mind, a state in strange contrast with
that in which I entered it, after my interview
with Mr. Worth.

"How I wish I had a clerkship in a first-class
mercantile or banking house," I muttered audibly
to myself. "I am not made for this kind of life,
and I can't stand it."

Just then, Mr. James Stokes, a leading broker,
overtook me. I had but a brief acquaintance
with him; but he placed his arm in mine in an
exceeding friendly manner.

"I understand you will soon bring out your
new company," he said, in a confidential tone.
"I think I may guess who your bankers are.
What I would say is, that our firm has peculiar
advantages in the management of such a stock,
and if you can arrange to give us the control of
it, we will make it all you can desire."

What should I reply? It was a risk to speak,

to be sure; but was I to make myself ridiculous by appearing ignorant of what Mr. Stokes meant? Doubtless this was the affair Deams had begged me to listen to, and which the shrewd broker had already got wind of.

Perceiving that I hesitated, Mr. Stokes continued: "You must not suppose I wish to commit you. Only when you are ready, think of what I tell you, and give me a call. Affairs have been very dull, but we shall have active times this fall, depend on it. Gold can't stand where it is. I am sorry to say so, very; but I must not act against my own convictions. Good-day."

"Gold can't stay where it is." The observation struck me with a strange and almost unearthly significance. I knew Mr. Stokes was one of the most loyal men in the Street, and had invariably discouraged attempts at speculation in gold. His present observation seemed to come from him without premeditation, yet as the result of an opinion audibly arrived at against his will. As I said, it produced the strongest impression on me.

It went down in my book with an ☞, which should recall it to my particular attention.

.   .   .   .

Punctual to his appointment, Deams was at my room at seven o'clock precisely.

"How lucky every thing seems to turn with you," was his first salutation. "I have seen Onis, and he told me Stokes, Mead & Co. think very highly of our scheme, and are ready to act as our brokers. What do you think of that, you unbeliever?"

I confess I was a good deal mollified at this remark, for I began to think there must be something of value after all in an enterprise which Mr. Stokes should go out of his way to speak to me about. I afterward learned the secret of his conduct. I could not, however, put away from my recollection the appearance of the three gentlemen whom I encountered at my office, and for whom I entertained such a repugnance.

"Yes," continued Deams, "we are at length all right. In fact, we are getting into shape

much more rapidly than I had myself calculated
on. In a few weeks, my boy, you may draw a
pretty large check on your bank, say with five
figures, and the only question the teller will ask
is: 'How will you have it?'"

Deams continued to rattle on in this stra n,
without any interruption from me. A very pleas-
ing vision was flitting before my mind, produced
by a momentary indulgence of the fancy.

"What if all these brilliant predictions prove
true? Who knows but you will suddenly realize
a fortune? Did not Alfred Johnson clear a
hundred thousand by bringing out the great
Nugget Bullion Company? Chester Symonds,
too:—he discovered a tin mine in New Hampshire, and sold out to Sparks, Hodge & Co. for
seventy-five thousand. Of course, it is not your
legitimate business man who undertakes these
things, but what of that? What matter how the
money is made, if honestly made? and if I do
make it!"

I held my breath unconsciously. A thought

7*

of Mary Worth was natural in this connection. Yes, indeed, if I do make it, I would seek her out, and the thought of the adieu she waved to me from her window made my heart beat audibly.

"What the deuce is the matter?"

It was the voice of Deams which recalled me to myself.

"I say, are your wits wool-gathering? What were you thinking of?" he exclaimed.

"Of that large check you were speaking about, with five figures in the margin."

"Good!" cried Deams, "I am glad you begin to have some appreciation of what I am doing for you. I shall expect an apology for your savage manner this morning."

"You shall have it, Deams, the moment my check is honored; and now let me have the promised explanation. First, what is your famous scheme, then who are your three 'friends,' and why did you represent me as a capitalist? How did Stokes come to know me in the matter at all?"

"One at a time, then," said Deams, "and first, can you tell me the price of coal?"

"No."

"I suppose not; but I can tell you it is nearly fifty per cent. higher than it has ever been before, with a prospect of a rising market."

"What of it? Neither you nor I are at housekeeping, and we do not intend to be for the present, I fancy."

"Look at that," cried Deams, with an air of triumph,—"see that."

He unrolled a large lithograph sheet, covered with many colored lines and sections. On one corner I read—

"*Map of coal lands belonging to Grover P. Wilcox, Esq., situated in Shawnee County, Pennsylvania, consisting of thirteen thousand seven hundred acres.*"

"Well?"

"Well," echoed Deams, "you have got control of that magnificent tract. I have arranged

all the details for the largest and most successful coal company ever originated in this city."

"Superior to Parker Vein?" I inquired dryly.

"Have done with your jesting," said Deams.
"This is the real thing. Property unsurpassed.
Veins fourteen feet in width, and inexhaus-
tible. Transportation, Shawnee Railroad to pass
right through it. Price, only a million and
a half of dollars. Three hundred thousand cash,
balance in stock of the company at par. Easy
terms of payment."

"And the three hundred thousand dollars,
cash payment?—"

"Runs over a space of five years—only sixty
thousand per annum."

"But, the first sixty thousand?"

"We shall go to the public for that," said
Deams. "Meantime, *you* are the capitalist. Do
you take?"

"No, I don't."

"Well, I did not suppose you would without further explanation, and to do that I must

show you the prospectus as soon as I have prepared it. To-morrow I shall fill up the list of the Trustees of the new company, and I will then open the whole budget. In a word, however, we have secured this property. A number of 'good' men are ready to take it up.

"You know," he continued, "there must always be some one to stand between the seller and the company, else there could be no '*ground floor.*' I have put you into that position, where I rather think you can take care of our interests. Now you see the value of a name free and clear. If you had any thing against you, it wouldn't do, you know, to hold the title."

I did see.

"Now, all I ask is," continued Deams, "that you say nothing which shall commit yourself till I have the papers ready to submit to you."

"But those disgusting wretches——"

"You mistake them, Powers. They are the gentlemen who introduced me to the property—acquaintances of Mr. Wilcox, the proprietor."

"Who help make the '·UNDERGROUND' below the '*ground floor*'—eh! 'a lower deep below the lowest deep,' I suppose?"

Deams turned very red in the face.

"You do not think——" he began.

"Oh, no, I don't think any thing, Deams, only this: if you have a fair case for a proper speculation, and want nothing *im*proper of me, why, I will go into it—that's all."

"Now, you talk like a rational man," said Deams.

"That's a little doubtful," I responded, "only don't attempt to humbug me."

"*I* attempt it," and Mr. Horace Deams assumed an air of desperate astonishment.

"One word more," I said. "That five hundred and fifty dollar note is due next week. Shall you be ready with your portion of the money?"

"Don't be in the least alarmed. I have already spoken to Mr. Masterman and told him

I should want a few hundred dollars, and he has promised I should have all I required."

"I am glad of it. You will not, on any account, disappoint me?"

"You may rely on me, positively," said Deams.

And thus the conference ended.

CHAPTER XVII.

The Worth family returned to town earlier than I anticipated.

On entering church the following Sabbath—I well recollect it was the third Sunday in September—I felt by a species of magnetism, electric affinity, odic force, call it what you will, that Mary Worth was in the house.

This was before I had looked toward the pew. My heart beat loudly. I hardly dared raise my eyes. At length I did raise them, and glanced in the direction of *her* seat.

She was there. I could not see her face, only the side of the hat which concealed it.

On the instant a delicious sense of repose stole over me; a feeling that whatever should come, or happen, all was right.

On my word, at that time I had no wish

or desire for any further acquaintance. I did not care even to speak to Mary Worth. To know that every week we should be seated near each other, under the same roof, was happiness enough.

Reader, this sounds desperately romantic and sentimental, does it not? Perhaps you think that my Wall Street delineations are to turn out mere lackadaisical vapors of the Pamela school.

I can not help it. I only say in reply that the person is, indeed, God forsaken who has lost his romance, and I, Henry Powers, declare to you I have not lost mine, and do not intend to lose it either.

Therefore, I repeat that what I say of my feelings for Mary Worth is true. I *did* feel just as I say I did, and I am not ashamed to own it.

Well, how is it with yourself, great Operator, or petty Schemer; millionaire, or poor devil; Wielder of immense power in finance, or desperate Shinner around the curb-stones from ten to three?

Tell me, each one of you, is there not something that breeds around your heart, and keeps you within the pale of humanizing emotions? A wife whom you love; a young girl to whom faith and truth are plighted; a mother or sister dependent on you; in short, *something*, or *somebody*, which touches your affections?

Man of money! *you* don't acknowledge this as you drive a hard bargain, or employ the power of your wealth to force a contract?

Poor devil! you confess to no such weakness, while you practice a miserable deception to raise the needful X, which *must*, in some way, be laid hold of. No, neither of you admit it while in the "Street," but you dare not deny it as you go homeward in the afternoon. Therefore you need not stop in the reading of my narrative, and affect to be disgusted at my sentimentality.

The services were over. As the crowd

swept into the center aisle I was brought close upon Mr. Worth, who bowed to me as usual.

I have omitted to state that after my interview with him in Wall Street, described in the last chapter, he never stopped me to shake hands, but was particular, however, always to bow after a peculiar manner—as one bows to an equal with whom one is well acquainted, but not on intimate terms. I enjoyed and felt flattered by this delicate mark of appreciation. "That man understands me, and wishes to let me know it," I said to myself.

So then, coming out of church, Mr. Worth turned and bowed after the style I have mentioned. Mrs. Worth walked a little in advance; she, too, took evident pains to salute me, and in a way that satisfied me her husband had given her an account of our late interview.

Mary Worth was still further on. She did not turn her head, and I got no glimpse of her face. But on going out I saw her standing in the vestibule, as if waiting my approach.

She did not stop for me to put in practice my plan of demeanor toward the Worth family, but, extending her hand, she exclaimed: "I am glad to see you, Mr. Powers, and to see you looking well. I do not think you had fully recovered when you left Long Branch, and I was very anxious about you, till papa met you, and told me you were really quite well again."

These words were spoken with such genuine earnestness that I was in great danger of breaking over the rule I had laid down for myself.

I stood looking straight into her eyes, and saying not a word. There was nothing in their expression which denoted anything beyond the natural and proper interest in one who had saved her life at the risk of his own—

" *Only this, and nothing more.*"

Her manner was neither confused nor timid —perhaps I should have been better satisfied had it been so—but frank and unhesitating.

All this flashed through my mind, in time

for me to recover, and reply in the same out-spoken, open manner. I said, "I was certainly entirely well again, and I hoped she was well, and was pleased to hear so through her father" —that was all.

During this scene, Mr. Worth and his wife stood near with complacent countenances, exhibiting no sign of impatience or of distrust.

Our little chat at an end, Mary Worth joined her parents and all walked away.

I noticed two or three young men eyeing me with a jealous air, and one or two young ladies turned quite round to take a look at me. I cared little for either. I felt sad, I hardly knew why. From that day I was to avoid further intercourse with Miss Worth—such was my determination—except the ordinary saluta-tions of courtesy.

CHAPTER XVIII.

THE next morning on going to my office, I found on my table a small paper slip which read as follows:

BANKING HOUSE OF ELI NICHOLS.

HENRY POWERS,

Your note for $550 is due 25th September.

The sight of this little printed reminder sent a cold shiver through me.

I was perfectly aware that my note fell due on that day, and was in Eli Nichols' hands: indeed, as the reader knows, I had already stirred Deams on the subject, and was doing every thing possible to scrape some money together myself.

Here, however, was something provokingly

tangible. It might be paraphrased in this way: "Remember, Henry Powers, that you have a note of five hundred and fifty dollars to pay to Eli Nichols on Saturday of this week!"

There was no mistaking it. It *must* be paid. After what had passed between me and old Eli, I think I would have submitted to any thing rather than fail to pay that note.

Why had I not followed the hint in my memorandum book, and been careful to keep my name "free and clear?"

I could have borrowed easily the few dollars I required, and now, as I begun to realize, I must provide for the two hundred and fifty dollars which Deams had undertaken to respond to.

In the midst of my cogitations that estimable gentleman entered the office.

I handed him the little "notice."

"Well," said Deams in an indifferent tone, "No fresh information here, I imagine. As the man in the play says: 'We knew it before.'"

"Certainly, but are you quite sure you will be ready on your part? Had you not better see your friend Masterman to-day about the money?"

"And provide Monday for Saturday!" retorted Deams. "Now I call that queer enough. I tell you, Masterman has promised me the money; I have informed him I should want it this week, and he would think it very odd for me to speak about it again."

"On the contrary, I should consider it very natural for you to tell him to-day that you are obliged to use the money Saturday; and then you have settled on a definite time, and he will have no excuse for disappointing you."

"Don't you know, my dear Powers," said Deams in an easy tone, "that every man has his own way in arranging these matters? You have your method; I have mine; and I don't think it of any advantage for either of us to lecture the other about how to manage with his friends."

Here the conversation dropped.

I confess I began to have but small hope that Deams could raise his share of the cash, notwithstanding the confidence he professed to place in the ability and good-will of Mr. Aaron Masterman.

I felt instinctively the absolute necessity of raising the amount myself; for the note once protested, I was satisfied that Eli Nichols, whom I had greatly incensed, would do all in his power to harrass me, and could at least greatly injure my credit in the Street.

"It is paying pretty dear for my first lesson," I said to myself; "but after all the loss of two hundred and fifty dollars shall never ruin Henry Powers: no, indeed!"

I had already made good my three hundred from some commissions on two or three notes which I had sold, for I found I should very likely have to starve while waiting on the immense fortune to be realized from the Coal Company, if I did not condescend to turn an honest penny in an honest though small way.

8

Deams, it is true, manifested a good deal of disgust at seeing me "trotting about," as he termed it, "chasing eighteen pence around the corner." I am happy to say his remonstrances had no effect on me; though the business of running from place to place, occupying a whole day, perhaps two days, in attempting to carve a trifling commission out of a piece of paper, while the seller insists on receiving so much, and the buyer will only give so much, is a very disgusting one.

I am sorry to record the fact that some of the larger brokers, when they see a respectable piece of paper, practice, for certain reasons, the habit of encouraging a belief that it can be disposed of at a much more favorable rate than the facts subsequently justify.

I remember that very day, there was a note for seventeen hundred and odd dollars, about four months to run, placed in my hands, made by a commercial house in good standing. Indeed, I will tell you, in confidence, the name of the house. It was that of Malcolm, Edgerton & Co., in South Street. The man who gave it to me, said, rather significantly, "The firm keeps their account in the Bank of Mutual Safety—you understand."

I did not, at the moment, understand, but shortly it occurred to me that the note was handed to me to negotiate from my supposed intimacy with Mr. Marmaduke Worth, the president.

"What are the terms?" I asked.

"Well," said my visitor, "no better note is made in New York: that you know. You know too, of course, as well as I, that at certain seasons this house puts out an immense quantity of paper, and then their notes stand a heavy shave,—have known it as high as two per cent. a month. But, without any chaffing, I can say you may take this and return the amount to me, less one and a half net, and make as much as you can out of it?"

I had no opportunity to reply, and probably

should have made none under any circumstances. I took the note, which was really all that the man had claimed for it, and proceeded to the well-known shop—I say "shop," for I consider that the proper name for it—of Peter T. Strain, which was not far from my own office. The principal himself happened to be in. I showed him the note.

"Ah, yes (in the blandest tones), about ten to twelve per cent., I suppose; yes, ten to twelve—twelve, as outside that will probably be the rate—prime note; still, you know, their paper rubs a little just at present. Step in, and let the book-keeper enter it."

Accordingly, I walked in, deposited the note, and left my name and address.

"When shall I call?"

"Some time in the course of the afternoon; or say to-morrow morning; my best customer who is in the habit of buying this paper has already been here, but I expect he will return again to-day."

I left the place thinking I should make a very good thing of the note of Malcolm, Edgerton & Co. I found my man waiting for me on going back to my office.

"Was he in? did you fix it?" he inquired, eagerly.

I was a little nettled. I did not relish being followed up so closely. .

"I can do nothing to-day," I said; "I hope to close it to-morrow."

"All right," was the response, "only my people want money badly. I will look in to-morrow."

I called pretty early the next day on Mr. Strain.

"Oh, I am very glad to see you,—was going to send in to your place. The gentleman who is in the habit of taking the Malcolm paper does not care to buy any more at present—thinks he has enough invested there. But understand me, there is no difficulty in selling the paper, none whatever, only we must submit to a little stiffer rate; that is what I wish to see you about. Shall we say twelve to fifteen, with fifteen as a limit?"

As "fifteen" was but one and a quarter per cent. a month, and I was to get "eighteen," or one and a half per cent., I said "yes" to Mr. Strain's suggestion, and begged him thereupon to expedite the affair.

"Certainly, certainly; call to-morrow, and I hope to have a check for you?"

Here was "to-morrow" again, but I submitted, and put my constituent off the best way I could for another day.

He was not quite content, but I gave him a strong assurance, and he departed.

My own profits were melting away, but I was now ambitious to carry the business through, and so I rendered myself in very good season next morning at the "shop."

Once more I was met by the bland and courteous Mr. Strain, and once more told that "fifteen" would not quite do, but he thought, in-

deed he believed he could say almost positively, that the offer of eighteen would bring the
money.

"I will advise you confidentially," he continued, "to accept the offer, for I am told there
will be another large amount on the market by
Saturday."

I was thoroughly indignant, but restrained my
wrath. "Mr. Strain, if you can discount the note
at one and a half to-day, I will take it. If you
are not sure of doing this before three, let me
have the note now."

"My dear sir," said Mr. Strain, mildly, "I do
say I feel confident of the offer, and for to-day—
you know I never buy notes myself; all on commission—all on commission; but call at two and
the money will be ready, I am entirely confident."

I quitted the place with the determination of
not returning to my own office till I had visited
Mr. Strain at two, for I had no disposition to
enter on a further explanation with the anxious

gentleman, who, I knew, was waiting for the money.

In this way I threw away the entire morning. "Never mind," I said: "It is true, I have lost a good deal of time and made nothing, but I shall have carried my point, and perhaps secured a customer."

At two o'clock I called on Mr. Strain, and received a check for the net proceeds of Messrs. Malcolm, Edgerton & Co.'s note. It was ready drawn, waiting my arrival. I expressed myself satisfied, and was turning to leave, when the book-keeper gave me a small strip with a memorandum as follows:

"Dis. Malcolm, E. & Co., $1,734 20
Coms. 1-4, $4 34."

"Excuse me," I said, hurriedly. I handed out five dollars, received sixty-six cents in change, and came away "silently," like the Arabs.

The joke was too good, so I only laughed at myself for being minus four dollars and thirty-four cents, besides about two days' gratuitous labor.

I had the discretion to deposit the money in the bank where I kept my account, and draw my own check for it; this done, I stepped quickly to my office, handed the check to my customer, who had been waiting since twelve o'clock, and was getting very red in the face. I apologized briefly for the delay, but in the tone of a man who feels himself to be strong.

The effect was evident.

"To-day is just as well, just as well, exactly," said he, "though we could not have got along very well *over* to-day, I admit. It takes a little time, I know, to turn to advantage. You have made a good thing out of it, that is, in a small way. There is some difference between seven per cent. and eighteen."

"I am content," said I, with a peculiar emphasis, which I will be bound my man did not understand, but which I felt.

Thereupon he took his leave.

8*

Perhaps you would like to know why I manifest so much indignation at the conduct of Mr.
Peter T. Strain. Was he not very frank in all
his explanations? Did he not account satisfacto-
rily for the delays, and, finally, did he not
promptly give the money at the very moment
promised; indeed, when he had not quite absolutely promised?

A word in your ear. Do not let this be
repeated, for Mr. Peter T. Strain's establishment
is highly respectable, and he himself a very cred-
itable member of the community. From desperate insolvency he has risen to great wealth.
He has a handsome house in town, and a beautiful country-seat in Westchester County, and all
from this one-quarter of one per cent. commission
on the notes which pass through his hands. So
he would have you suppose.

After this, will you believe me when I tell
you that Peter T. Strain never offered the note
of Malcolm, Edgerton & Co. for sale at all during the three days he was finessing with me;

never offered it at all until after he had given me a check for the amount agreed on? Then he doubtless placed it at about ten per cent. per annum with some customer who relied on his judgment.

It was nothing *very* bad, you know. Peter T. Strain was too respectable to cheat me—much. Besides, he only deals in first or second class paper, and never descends to vulgar shaves. Peter T. Strain is not a bad man—out of the Street. He is a "good husband and a kind father," and a "very liberal person."

In his "shop" he is a knave, and nothing else. Why?

.   .   .   .

This was Thursday, and quite the close of the day. Deams had not spoken to me about the note since our Monday's conversation. He appeared very busy, however, with his "prospectus." His "three friends"—Mr. Aaron Masterman, Mr. Elton Pope, and Mr. Philo Coldbrook —came in to see him on two several occasions.

On Friday I ventured to speak to Deams again. Had he asked Mr. Masterman for the money? and if not, I begged he would do so at once, that I might be relieved from apprehension.

Deams changed countenance slightly. "It's a deuced pity, Powers, that we can't manage to throw the thing over for another week."

"For what reason?"

"Why, I am just at a point with Masterman which makes it a little awkward, you see, to ask him to lend me. Don't you perceive?"

"I can't say I do. On the contrary, you told me you had actually engaged the money from him for this week. He has already promised you the amount, has he not?"

"Well, yes, indirectly."

"What makes you say 'indirectly,' Deams, when you told me decidedly that he promised to let you have the money?" I exclaimed in an irritated tone.

"Now, if you insist on it, Powers, I *will* borrow it, but I beg you to hold off if possible for just one week more."

"*I* hold off! I should rather think Eli Nichols is the man to be consulted on that head."

"Just the thing," said Deams, "I can renew it with him for fifteen days easy enough, and then we *shall* be out of the woods."

"Not with my consent."

"Pshaw! don't talk nonsense! Just pay what you have on hand, and, by George, we can renew like a knife for two hundred and fifty."

"What has become of your tender regard for my credit?" I said, with a sneer.

"Please don't talk in that way, when you know I am bending every effort to securing a fortune for us both. You know, Mr. Powers, I have thought of nothing else all summer. For heaven's sake, don't ask me to injure myself with our new friends."

"How much can you do toward your part?" I asked, calmly.

"Well, you see, Powers, my expenses have been

rather large lately. I have had to entertain these gentlemen on several occasions, for we must keep up appearances, you know."

"Which means you do not intend to help me with a dollar."

"It means that, literally, I *can* not," said Deams, in a deprecatory tone.

I had recovered my temper. Really, I was not much disappointed, and it was useless to exhibit any idle ebullition.

"Had you told me this, Deams," I said quietly, "at first, instead of ——"

"Don't reproach me: I feel worse about it than you do, and will get the note renewed if you will let me, or do anything you tell me to. In fact," continued Deams, starting from his seat, "you need not pay it at all if you say so, it was a cursed cut-throat usurious transaction, and the old screw can't recover a dollar. Let him sue and be ——"

"We will say no more about it, Deams;" and I left the office, very much to his relief, I fancy.

I felt myself in a bad way, as I walked down the street. "What are my prospects? Let me look them in the face. At five and twenty, with good health, a good education, a thorough knowledge of commercial business, and an untiring energy, I bid fair to settle down into a petty note broker, or what is worse, a schemer in bubble companies."

I believe I have not mentioned a Mr. Holman, who was a junior partner in the house of Gardner, Lynde & Co. when I was with that firm. He was but five or six years older than I, and was an agreeable, companionable man. While Mr. Gardner was in Europe making an effort to settle with the creditors of the concern, Mr. Holman had engaged in some Government contract, in which, being an incorruptibly honest man, it was quite impossible for him to make any thing beyond a respectable living.

His wife had a snug little sum in her own right, and so he was altogether in very comfortable circumstances.

I resolved to call and see him, and ask him to lend me the two hundred and fifty dollars. He was still a young man, and I did not doubt his entire sympathy with me.

I found him at his place of business, and alone. Without delay or circumlocution I explained how I had been caught, and asked him to help me to the required sum.

"I have not got the amount in hand," he said, "but I can borrow it. I perceive of how much importance it is to you, and I will see that you have the money," he said promptly.

What different types of men we encounter! Look at Eli Nichols: look at Deams: look at Mr. Holman. Why can't all the world be honest and kind and good? and what are those other creatures made for?

Such was my soliloquy as I left Mr. Holman's place, after receiving a cordial invitation from him to call and talk over affairs, the state of the country, and so forth.

The next day, before twelve o'clock, Mr. Holman sent me a check for two hundred and fifty dollars.

I said nothing about it to Deams, nor he to me. Indeed, I doubt very much if he gave the matter a thought after he had fairly saddled it on me.

I at once had my own check certified for the amount of my note, five hundred and fifty dollars, and as Deams had made it payable at my office, I sat and quietly waited for it to be sent in.

About half-past two who should enter but old Eli himself! It was quite out of the business course, as it was the duty of a clerk to present the note. Doubtless the old fellow wished to witness my mortification, if not able to pay. I afterward learned that he had previously sent and ascertained I was in.

The old fellow advanced stoutly to the desk where I was sitting and placed the note before my eyes. I took the certified check from the drawer and placed it quietly before his eyes.

Eli looked chopfallen. He picked up the

check, turned and left the room without a word
being spoken on either side.

I counted the man my enemy after this; but
I was mistaken. He had not the capacity to be
a friend of anybody, but he rather admired the
way I treated him—payment of the note included
—and I frequently heard of his passing encomiums
on me in his rough, vulgar way, such as that I
would "*do*:" the man who would get ahead of
me "must get up early," and the like.

All this because I had refused to be made
his tool, and had been prompt in meeting my ob-
ligations.

CHAPTER XIX.

I AM about to give you another phase of my Wall Street experience. Thus far, reader, you must have felt dissatisfied, if not disgusted, with the petty scope of my proceedings.

You have looked, doubtless, for some record which should amply sustain your notions of the magnitude of "Street" operations, and explain how, as if by magic, men and things change like resolving and dissolving views.

Behold me, then, an active inquirer into the famous coal scheme which Deams has introduced to me, and which is represented by the solid house of Masterman, Coldbrook & Pope.

Do you ask me why I consented even to examine the affair, when I so thoroughly knew the character of Deams by actual observation, and felt that I knew equally well, by intuition, the status of Masterman, Coldbrook and Pope?

I can only say in reply that I was allured insensibly by the dazzling idea of somehow or other "making a strike." Other enterprises which had turned out well had been started in weak and often doubtful hands, yet ultimately found their proper place on the market and settled on a solid and respectable basis.

Mind, I was only committed to "look into" the affair. But Deams knew, and his "three friends" knew, which I did not, that this was tantamount to enlisting me in it.

I had afterward to learn that the apothegm "to hesitate and parley is to be lost" will bear many applications, none more true than with reference to such transactions.

One morning—time has carried us on to the middle of October, with little or no change in my own matters, only that I was living, more than ever, perhaps, from hand to mouth—one morning, I say, Deams announced to me that he was ready to go "fully into details" on the subject of the Great Coal Company, and that for the purpose of being quite uninterrupted he thought we had better go round to the establishment of Masterman, Coldbrook & Pope, where every document could be seen and all questions answered "by the book."

"I thought we were first to look over the papers together before admitting any one to the interview," I said tartly.

"So we are, Mr. Powers, but we shall have a private room quite to ourselves, and since all the books, papers, reports, specimens, and so forth, are at Masterman's, I think we can't do better than go there."

It was impossible to say a word against so plain a proposition; accordingly we started together to visit the "establishment" (so Deams always called it) of Masterman, Coldbrook & Pope.

Perhaps I should state that ever since the affair of the note, Deams had treated me with a good deal of deference.

Whether his object was merely to flatter me,

or whether he inferred from the circumstances of my paying the five hundred and fifty dollars so promptly that I had funds in reserve, it is of little purpose to inquire. He certainly was much more respectful in his manner than ever before, and now said, " *Mr.* Powers," when addressing me, instead of the more familiar, " Powers."

" What business are these people in," I asked, as we passed along.

" Well, they have now opened very fine offices for the purposes of the company, as well as for their own use, so that the company can commence at once, you perceive, with superior accommodations."

Deams had an odd habit of saying, " You perceive," whenever any thing was a little obscure, or when he was not prepared to afford explanations.

Thinking I should shortly be able to "perceive" for myself, I made no reply, but marched on in silence.

" Here we are," said Deams, stopping before one of the finest buildings in the street.

We mounted one flight of stairs only, when I saw over the door in front of me, in large letters :

HOPE AND ANCHOR

MUTUAL COAL COMPANY.

HORATIO J. DEMPSEY, *President.*

On the door I read :

MASTERMAN, COLDBROOK & POPE,

BANKERS.

There was no time for further queries—Deams entered, and I followed him into the main room, which was protected from intruders by a line of counters and iron railing, with two or three small spaces in the latter to admit conference if desired.

Over a small archway, in the center, I read : *Cashier;* at another, *Transfer Clerk;* and so on.

At one of these interesting points, I observed the protruding nose of Mr. Elton Pope, and caught a glimpse of his carroty wig.

He looked littler, and his nose larger than ever, as he bobbed his head in token of welcome.

Deams did not wait for any further demonstration, but walked to a side door which opened into a cozy room, where we found a pleasant fire; the day was cool; and sitting before it Mr. Aaron Masterman, who was busily occupied reading a long advertisement in one of the daily papers.

He rose as we entered, shook hands with Deams cordially, and with me in a deferential style, which was quite overcoming.

"That will do, I guess," he said, handing the paper to Deams, as he placed his thick forefinger on the notice.

The latter made a careless assent, scarcely looking at the article in question.

"Mr. Powers has consented to give us an hour or two this morning for examination and conference, before investing in our enterprise or undertaking to interest his friends in it. May I trouble you for the title papers and the contract held by your firm, also the report of Professor Silex, and of Dr. Quartz, besides the various letters relating to the property."

"Certainly, sir," said Mr. Masterman. "I will speak to Mr. Pope, and you will have them before you without a moment's delay."

He left the apartment, and thereupon I took occasion to look about me.

The room was elegantly carpeted, and furnished in the most handsome manner.

On one side was a rosewood cabinet filled with various mineralogical specimens, admirably selected, many of which were rare. A shelf was entirely devoted to "Specimens of coal from the lands of Grover P. Wilcox, Esq." These were remarkably fine ones, and ought certainly to have satisfied the most critical and fastidious examiner.

"It looks all right, don't it?" said Deams confidently.

I made no reply.

"Splendid cabinet: it belongs to Professor

9

Quartz. We have borrowed it for the season. Good idea, don't you think so?"

I had no time to make any observation, for the door opened and Mr. Elton. Pope came in with his arms filled up to the end of his long proboscis, with several immense books, maps, newspapers, printed pamphlets, and divers rolls of manuscript.

The little man stood for a moment as if doubtful how to get rid of his load, each eye wandering restlessly from point to point, as if quite independent of the other.

"Let me relieve you, my dear sir," said Deams, and he proceeded gradually to unload the poor fellow, who, when the operation was concluded, bowed, in the most touching manner, to me, and turned and left the room.

"Now for work," said Deams, taking up one of the large volumes, which I saw was marked "Geological Survey of the State of Pennsylvania."

"What is all this for?" I asked.

"I wish," continued Deams, with an innocent air, "to show you the immense value of the coal deposits of the State of Pennsylvania."

"Don't make an ass of yourself, Deams, or attempt to make a fool of me," I said, in an angry tone. "If you have any wish to talk business, why, proceed; if not, I'm off."

"Now, then, don't flash in this way, when I am doing my best to please you. The fact is, one never knows where you will break out next. I thought, of all things, you would like it if I began at the beginning, and now my sincere desire to suit you puts you in a passion."

Deams had a singular power of mollifying wrath, at least with me. The innocent simplicity he assumed was so ludicrous that I laughed in spite of myself.

"Shall we take up the titles to the Wilcox Estate?" he inquired in the same tone.

"I am no lawyer, Deams, and I suppose your counsel has already passed on them."

"That is true; Joel P. Phillips, a distinguished

lawyer, has examined the papers and pronounced them all right. His opinion should satisfy anybody."

"What next?"

"Next, if you please, are very particular details of the properties, with maps and descriptions of the different veins.

"Look here," continued Deams, producing a pamphlet of about one hundred pages, containing maps covered with sections of the different veins.

The pamphlet also embraced the reports of Professor Silex and Dr. Quartz, besides numerous letters from practical men who were more or less known to me.

"I am willing to call this 'all right,' as you term it, Deams; so let us come to the actual matter in hand. Let me see your scheme, then I will tell you how far I am willing to co-operate with you."

"Here is the Prospectus," said Deams.

I took it and read as follows:—

Hope and Anchor Mutual Coal Company, established under the act of the State of New York, passed Feb. 17, 1848. Capital $2,750,000, divided into 550,000 shares of $5 each. *This company is organized on the plan of enabling each shareholder to become the producer of his own coal, and each share of stock entitles the holder to one ton of coal a year at cost.*

President,
HORATIO J. DEMPSEY.

Vice President,
ELIHU PRICE PETERS.

Treasurer,
AARON H. MASTERMAN.

Secretary,
ELTON POPE.

Trustees,

HORATIO J. DEMPSEY, Antartic Iron Mills.

ELIHU PRICE PETERS (Peters & Osterhaus).

AARON H. MASTERMAN (Masterman, Coldbrook & Pope).

JOHN R. STILLHOUSE (Stillhouse, Fleet & Co).
DAVID BROKAW, United Steam Wire Co.
ELTON POPE (Masterman, Coldbrook & Pope).
HENRY POWERS, Banker.

Bankers,
Bank of Mutual Safety,
MASTERMAN, COLDBROOK & POPE.

Counsel,
JOEL P. PHILLIPS, ESQ. ; ERASTUS EAMS, ESQ.

Geologist.—Prof. PAOLI SILEX.

Practical do.—Dr. RUFUS QUARTZ.

I sat and looked at the names in perfect amazement.

With the exception of Masterman, Pope, and myself, these names were as well known and respectable as any in New York. Indeed, so perfectly was I taken by surprise at the sight of them, that, at first, I never thought of the unwarrantable use made of my own name.

After I recovered a little, it occurred to me that the others might have been placed there, as mine had been, without consulting the parties concerned.

Deams watched me in silence.

At length I looked up. "Tell me," I said, "are these names here with the consent of the persons indicated?"

"Every one of them, on my honor," said Deams, stoutly, "except your own."

"And why did you not consult me?" I asked.

"I will tell you why, Mr. Powers. It is because you are so very queer sometimes, so very queer. One can never tell what you are going to do or what you will say, and I candidly confess to you, now we are all strait, that I was afraid to let you know about it—indeed I was."

"But why do you put me on at all?"

"Now don't, I beg," said Deams, laughing, "don't try to look simple, as if you didn't know as much about some things as the next man. I say," he continued, "do you see my name there?"

"No."

"I should rather suppose not. Yet am I not the life and soul of the enterprise, the originator, developer, promoter, and so forward. Are you not my ally, associate, and friend, and at the same time entirely competent to represent, care for, and protect our interests in the Hope & Anchor Mutual Coal Company?"

Deams evidently had gained considerable courage since the list of trustees was completed, which made him particularly grandiloquent on this occasion.

"Honestly, then, without prevarication, you declare these individuals have consented to act as trustees?" I said very seriously.

"I do," replied Deams.

"Well, then, now for the scheme."

"Now for it," echoed Deams in a business tone. "Let us keep our wits about us, Mr. Powers, and we have made all the money we shall require for the rest of our lives; let me tell you that."

"Never mind that, now, Deams, but give me the programme."

"Here you have it. First, you understand the principle on which we propose to run the machine—the mutual principle, I mean?"

"Yes, I believe I do, and what is more I think the principle a first-rate one. In my opinion, if honestly conducted, it will take well."

"Aha! I thought you would come to it," said Deams triumphantly. "I invented the idea myself. I was brought to it, partly by seeing notices of the high price of coal, but more particularly by reading lots of newspaper articles, abusing the retailers.

"If every newspaper had been under pay, they could not have served the Hope and Anchor better. No, indeed; everybody is crying out against the coal dealers, and the public are ready to go in for any thing which will bring the rascals to terms.

"On this hint I spake, as Othello says, and you see how I have got on. Besides, I came the benevolent dodge, which secured Mr. Dempsey for President. You know he is great on taking care of the city poor. He is interested in a dozen different societies. We are going to supply the whole of them with coal at cost. Poor folks shall be victimized no longer.

"With Dempsey once in, you may judge it was not difficult to get Stillhouse, his son-in-law. The rest followed like sheep."

"Then you have all the funds you want?"

"Why, not exactly. You see all these good sort of people are just as ready to make money as the other kind; why shouldn't they be? So I explained to Mr. Dempsey that we had reserved for him two thousand shares of stock, as compensation for his services, and that we should not call on him for any money. So we say to all the trustees. Mr. Dempsey was content. He consented to act, but declined to keep the stock for himself; he said he would hold it, however, for the poor of the Five Points. Noble fellow, that!"

" How are you to get money then," I asked.

" From the public, sir, on this prospectus! Let me explain."

And thereupon Deams went into the figures, which I propose shall be the subject of the next chapter.

CHAPTER XX.

MARY WORTH!

Reader you have these cabalistic—to me cabalistic—words placed at the head of this chapter, instead of the "figures" which were promised you of the magnificent scheme of the HOPE & ANCHOR MUTUAL COAL COMPANY!

In this connection you doubtless consider it quite out of place, just as you are seated at the table with Deams and myself, your wits sharpened for the trial, to have only these two words put on the programme!

"It satisfies me," you say pettishly, "that Powers will never succeed." Besides, you feel, perhaps, that I am trifling with you; or, you imagine, on consideration, I don't deem it prudent to let you into the affair, and you call this very shabby treatment after my holding out so many inducements to attract your attention.

Suppose it to be so; what have you to complain of? Are we not in Wall Street? Have we passed our words to each other? Jones, having taken up my enterprise *without* examination, while you, Robinson, are wasting precious time *in* examining it, has secured the right to a "call" of the stock at a favorable rate, thus shutting you out from a participation in this magnificent and colossal enterprise.

After this, Robinson, think quick, and strike quick, or you will not do for the "Street."

However, on this occasion, I admit I am alarming you without cause. The matter is still "open."

Let me say my say about Mary Worth, and then to business.

In the midst of these figures, how came her name interposed?

I will tell you. It happened, just as I was setting myself to the work of investigation, that something whispered, "Succeed in this, and you will win *her!*"

And was it not impossible for me to become
her suitor without first acquiring a fortune, or
at least a competency?

No, it was not possible, because not consistent with self-respect.

I knew very well several young men about
town, who were always on the look out for
rich girls. There is Trovers, who was for fifteen
years, as I have been told, indefatigable in his
attempts to obtain a rich wife [you know Trovers, lately a teller in this same Bank of Mutual
Safety], and only last year accomplished his
object—secured a young widow with two hundred thousand. But everybody points at Trovers, and calls him disagreeable names. To be
sure he has quit the bank, and set up an establishment, and goes into "society;" still I
doubt if any one respects him. Besides, although
scarcely a year married, people say he and his
wife do not live happily together. He does
not care, it is true, but *I* should care, and so
I could never place myself in his position.

"If I make a fortune, I shall feel satisfied to cultivate an acquaintance with Miss Worth, and attempt to win her. Otherwise not." So I said to myself after returning from Long Branch.

When, therefore, some spirit whispered in my ear the words I have just recorded, it made my pulse beat very quick, so that I breathed with difficulty, when I thought what was possible to come of the morning's work which was before me.

CHAPTER XXI

"Now, Mr. Powers, I am going to act on the square with you," said Deams, with the courageous air of a man who had just adopted a virtuous resolution.

"So I suppose."

"Yes, you shall have the whole story. What I know, you shall know. We will work like two brothers, and divide even."

"Well?"

"Well," continued Deams, "this affair is all MINE. Those chaps in there (pointing to the other room) are mere——"

"Tools of yours; I thought as much," interrupted I.

"No, no, Mr. Powers, I was not going to say 'tools' but agents; they are my agents—well, not exactly agents either; in fact, I got the affair up, and they do as I say."

"I think you had better let my application stand, Deams.   Go on."

"You see," continued Deams, "I have known Pope for several years.   He keeps a small hat and cap store in Sixth Avenue.   Very honest fellow is Pope, very snug too, has laid by four or five thousand cash.

"Now Pope knew Grover P. Wilcox, the owner of the coal land, and one day was mentioning the subject to me, and how Wilcox would like to sell.

"I turned it over in my mind, and finally told Pope that if Wilcox would go to the expense of a map, and have the property reported on by Quartz and Silex, I would take it up, provided we could agree on the terms.   Well, we came to an agreement (between us, Powers, only between us)," exclaimed Deams, convulsingly, as he grasped my hand in token of the confidence he was reposing in me, "which was, I say, that I should pay Wilcox sixty thousand dollars cash for the entire property."

"Sixty thousand dollars!" I said in amazement. "Why, Deams, you go to the public
with a statement that we pay a million and a
half of dollars. Three hundred thousand dollars
in cash, and the balance in stock of the Company
at par."

"I beg your pardon, Mr. Powers. I do not
say *we* do any such thing. I say the *Company*
pays that amount for the property, and so it
does and so it will, or my name isn't Deams."

"That's what I call rascality," I said with
emphasis.

"You are a fool, Powers, and nothing else,"
exclaimed Deams, thrown out of his sense of
propriety by my rather startling proposition.

"Hold on," he continued, seeing my face
flush, "hold on, and let me ask you a question
or two. Suppose you had a chance to buy a
lot up town for a thousand dollars, and you
knew at the same time you could sell it in
sixty days for two thousand, would you make
the purchase?"

"Very likely."

"Then you see no objection to buying at one price and selling at a better one, provided you use no deception?"

"No."

"Well, then, where is the 'rascality' in this case? Wilcox has a very large tract of what is now to him wild land. It probably cost him a mere song twenty years ago, or he may have inherited it. He has no knowledge of the machinery of getting up a company to work his mines. We have. So he furnishes the raw material at a low figure. We buy, and get the price it should really command when properly developed. I don't suppose you are so very benevolent as to wish to work for the public exactly for nothing?"

"I admit, Deams, there is a good deal in what you say," I remarked, considerably softened, "but it is the tremendous difference between the price we pay and the price it is put in at to the Company, that staggers me."

"Now stop just there," said Deams; "stick a pin there. You admit my principle is correct, only you fear I overcharge the Company for the property. What if I show you, by proper computations and by certificates of first-class men, that we are *not* overcharging, it is all right, is it not?"

"Let the matter rest where it is, Deams, and go on with your explanation." I felt that he had the best of the argument, but I was not altogether convinced either.

"I will resume," said Deams pompously. "But I beg you, Mr. Powers, not to interrupt me again with objections until I am through; then raise as many as you please."

I was silent, and Deams proceeded.

"Let me see, where was I? oh, I was saying I had agreed to pay sixty thousand dollars cash for the property. So far, so good. Then came the organization, where to begin and how to do it. That is, how to get the property honestly—mind you, I say *honestly*—to the Company at our price.

"Once deciding that it is worth all the Company is asked to pay for it, the only question is, you perceive, the mere manipulation. Pope, was acquainted with Coldbrook. They are first cousins. Coldbrook is in the hosiery line, and he too has some money. Neither of these gentlemen are particularly presentable, as you have doubtless observed, but they are straightforward, honest fellows; they mean right, and will do just as they agree.

"As to Masterman, I have known him a good while. He used to be knocking about the Street ten years ago; he went off to California, and turned up here about three months since. He knows the ropes and will do what I tell him."

"How about *his* honesty?"

"I entreat you not to interrupt me," repeated Deams. "You make me lose the thread of— let me see—oh, I was about saying that Pope at-

tends the same church with Horatio J. Dempsey,
and is a very active person in all that is going on.   Helps look up orphan children, calls on
the indigent families,—in fact, does a great deal
of good.

"Just as soon as I thought of the benevolent idea of furnishing coal to the poor at cost,
without regard to their taking stock, I told
Pope he must secure Mr. Dempsey for President;
that he must urge it on him as a matter of
duty.   The thing took splendidly—Dempsey was
delighted.   He was cautious enough, too.   He
had a formal interview with Quartz and Silex,
and insisted that his own counsel, Mr. Phillips,
should certify as to the titles, before he consented to act.

"Of course we asked him for no money, and
donated two thousand shares all round.

"So far all was successful.   Next came the
bargain with my friends.

"I wanted them to open a 'banking house,'
where the office of the Company should be

located. It would cost at least a thousand dollars to furnish it; besides, the rent is fearfully high, but I considered it essential to success.

"At length we agreed on the following: Wilcox was to give Masterman, Coldbrook, and Pope a contract for the sale of the property to *them*, which was to be laid before the Company, and for which contract the Company are to pay the aforesaid Masterman, Coldbrook, and Pope, the sum of twelve thousand dollars cash, and assume the entire responsibility of carrying it out.

"This twelve thousand our three friends are to divide; but in consideration of that, they hire these offices and furnish them. They get, besides, a hundred thousand dollars apiece of the stock, after the Company is in full mining operation—not before."

Deams paused to take breath, and to see what effect his recital had on me.

"Go on," I said, quietly.

Deams did not go on, but instead, he continued silent. He looked for a while very hard at me, as if trying to satisfy himself of the impression he had made.

At length he broke out as follows: "Powers —one word—we know each other well, or ought to. What I want to say is, if you are not willing to go into this with me, you will do nothing to my prejudice, will you?"

I answered at once—"Certainly not."

"I knew you wouldn't, my dear fellow, I knew you wouldn't. You are true as steel. I always felt you were. As to our Company, it is *right*. You may depend on it, and if you will let me, I will make an independent fortune for you."

"Go on, Deams," I repeated. "I certainly shall not decide against the scheme until I have heard you through."

"Thank you, my boy, thank you," said Deams, in a grateful tone. "Now let me have your attention to these figures."

Thereupon Deams placed a sheet of paper before me, and, drawing his chair near, pointed with his pencil to the schedule, which read as follows:—

HOPE AND ANCHOR.

Capital stock........................$2,750,000

Set aside for working capital.......... 1,250,000

    Remaining......................$1,500,000

Masterman, C. & P., 100,000

    each.....................$300,000

Four other parties, $10,000 each 40,000

For the press................ 100,000

Six benevolent clergymen...... 60,000

Broker....................... 100,000

Incidentals.................. 100,000

                    ——— 700,000

To be divided between Deams and

    Powers in stock................. $800,000

To be received in cash in five install-

    ments.............................. $300,000

To be paid Wilcox................ 60,000

Cash to be divided between Deams and

    Powers............................. $240,000

10

"What do you think of that? Say, now— what do you think of that, Powers? Four hundred thousand dollars of the stock apiece! Eighty thousand shares! Why, I tell you, they will go off like hot cakes, at two dollars a share, which means a clear one hundred and sixty thousand dollars each, cash, besides our yearly cash receipts of sixty thousand dollars for four years, making——"

"Deams, what do you wish me to *do* for being allowed to participate in this?"

"Always suspicious," replied Deams, with entire good-humor. "I have already explained that my name must not appear in this, because I am tabooed, financially. I want you to represent my interest and your own; besides, you are active, competent, and can be trusted. There, you have it."

I sat five minutes without making the least reply. Deams, meantime, was careful not to interrupt me.

My thoughts, if put into language, would run

something in this way. " I have a sort of innate conviction that this affair is all wrong—I can't exactly argue it out either. I only *feel* it. Still, am I not too straight-laced in my notions— Deams's scheme is the ordinary one for speculative companies—which often pay well and do well, and finally become remunerative. I am sorry I have taken such a dislike to his ' three friends'—I dare say, though, I do Pope and Coldbrook injustice. Deams says they are honest men. Doubtless they are. Masterman, unmistakably, is a hard case. However, I won't judge from appearances, at least not hastily. What is the necessity of judging at all? If such men as Dempsey, Peters, Stillhouse, and Brockaw have gone into this and indorsed the scheme to the public by consenting to act as trustees, why, Henry Powers, do you hesitate? Four first-class New Yorkers lead the enterprise, not you. ' Be not righteous overmuch.' I don't exactly know what that means, but it must mean something. Does n't it mean, Henry Powers, you can safely leave the morality of this scheme to those four excellent persons, and do your best to co-operate with them? . . . . . . Four hundred thousand dollars in stock. . . . . . . One hundred and sixty thousand dollars in money . . . Thirty thousand dollars a year cash for four years. . . . Wealth. . . . . . . Commanding position. . . . . Mary Worth!"

.   .   .   .

" Deams ?"

" What ?"

" I will go in!"

" Good.   I knew you would when you thought it over."

" Very well, I *have* thought it over.   Now let me know what your plan is for raising the money—that is the first point."

"Of course it is.   I will tell you my difficulty, and why I introduced you as the capitalist.   The twelve thousand dollars which I have promised to these people, they are getting a little restive about.   The fact is, Pope and Coldbrook have

furnished the offices, and the concern has rented
them, and the whole will count up a pretty figure. I have told them *you* would advance the
twelve thousand dollars as soon as you were satisfied, and so forth. Now you have entered on
the examination you can take a little time for it
—eh ?"

" Deams ?"

" What ?"

" How much of the twelve thousand dollars
goes to you? Recollect you are on the square
with me."

" One-fourth of it—three thousand dollars," responded Deams, with the contortion of a man
undergoing the extraction of an eye-tooth.

" One-half of which is mine."

" Certainly "—another tooth drawn.

" Well, Deams, that was very thoughtful in
you to provide for a little ready money."

" Wasn't it though !" said Deams, still wincing.

" How do you propose to procure this twelve
thousand dollars ?"

"I am a little uncertain. I did think *you* would raise it through the Bank of Mutual Safety, but I suppose there is no use asking you to do that?"

I shook my head.

"Do you propose any thing?" continued Deams.

"I do. Let us put the matter into the hands of a first-class broker, and raise what money we want through him. We will double the amount of stock he is to receive, if necessary. I will speak to Stokes myself about it."

"Will you?" said Deams, brightening up. "That is just what I was going to ask you to do. The whole thing is clear. Now I think we may call in our friends from the other room."

CHAPTER XXII.

AARON MASTERMAN, Elton Pope, and Philo Coldbrook were anxiously awaiting in the counting-room of their showy "banking-house," the result of my examination into the affairs of the new Company. Each had a particular interest in this. Masterman was impatient to handle his share of the twelve thousand dollars, while Pope and Coldbrook were beginning to tremble, as well they might, for their investment in so much fine furniture, and for their liability on account of so much rent and clerk hire.

Deams proceeded to open the door, and in a trice the firm of "Masterman, Coldbrook & Pope" entered.

"I am happy to announce to you, gentlemen," said Deams, in a pompous tone, "that my friend, Mr. Powers, has made very considerable progress in looking into our matters. He authorizes me to say, that he has no doubt he will bring the examination to a favorable conclusion. That done, I am further instructed to observe that the little sum you require, on passing the contract, will be forthcoming."

Here Deams looked toward me, as if seeking some token of acquiescence.

The "three friends," at the same time, turned their ardent gaze in my direction, while breathlessly waiting a confirmation of the welcome intelligence.

"Gentlemen," I said, "I am not very rapid in such matters, but I think I have seen enough of your scheme to warrant me in saying I have no doubt I shall take it up, and you will find me prompt in whatever I do undertake. I hardly think you can expect more from me to-day."

"Perfectly satisfactory," exclaimed Mr. Masterman, who acted as a sort of *claqueur* for the other two, "perfectly satisfactory. Speaks like a trump!"

"Very satisfactory, truly," said little Mr. Pope.

"Indeed it is," echoed Coldbrook.

"That being the case," said Deams, "suppose we have lunch. Masterman, let Abram order some lamb-chops, and a tenderloin, with the et ceteras, from Hinckley's, and seeing it is Mr. Powers' first visit to our office, why, two or three bottles of champagne won't come amiss."

Masterman bustled out to give the order, while Pope and partner manifested a very amiable assent, certainly,—considering the disbursements for the repast were to come from their treasury.

Two of Hinckley's waiters speedily appeared, and very soon the table of the "Board of Trustees of the Hope and Anchor Mutual Coal Company" presented a very inviting appearance.

Deams was now in his element. Visions of a "splendid success" grew more and more vivid as each successive bumper of champagne was tossed down.

Masterman was no way behind Deams in his practical appreciation of the article. In fact,

10*

these two worthies rather monopolized the three bottles. I think little Mr. Pope and lank Mr. Coldbrook were helped to a glass each only.

For myself, I partook of the lunch and the wine with considerable relish. I had a good opportunity to judge of the company I was keeping. "*In vino veritas*," you know; and I was pleased to be able to reconsider the hasty judgment I had previously formed of Pope and Coldbrook. I was convinced they were really honest persons, who had been carried away with the hope of rapidly making a fortune, and who had actually been made to believe, through the agency of Deams, that they were fitted for Wall Street operations.

As to Masterman, he simply developed, as he guzzled the wine, the characteristics I had previously given him credit for.

The hilarious occasion could not last forever. All things mundane must have an end.

Our little company at length broke up. Every one, myself included, expressing the opinion that we were on the road to fortune, if not to fame.

"Possibly to *notoriety*," something whispered.

I checked the mentor.

"I am in for it, and will go through," I muttered, as I turned down the street.

CHAPTER XXIII.

The next day, on coming down town, I stopped in to look at some offices which were to let in a central position in Wall Street.

These consisted of two small, but neat and handsomely furnished rooms, in the second story. The occupant had taken, originally, a five years' lease of them; and having been fortunate in business, was now going to Europe, leaving eighteen months of the term unexpired. I found the price reasonable, and I secured the rooms on the spot,

I next proceeded to a sign-painter, where I ordered a fine large sign, which should be placed over the door and running its entire width.

On this sign I directed to be painted in gilt letters :

HENRY POWERS.

Two or three small tin signs for the outside of the building and the passage-way completed the arrangements.

I made no specifications after my name, but stood before the public simply as "HENRY POWERS." It struck me that as long as I could claim no particular occupation, I had better let the name rest on its merits. "HENRY POWERS," standing by itself was rather imposing than otherwise. "HENRY POWERS, Stock-Broker," was altogether insignificant.

These arrangements concluded, I went to my old office, twisted off the tin sign—which was stuck on one side of the door, and in its place affixed a sheet of paper, on which was written:

Henry Powers, removed to No. —— Wall Street.

While I was inside collecting the few papers which belonged to me, Deams suddenly entered. Consternation was pictured on his countenance—

"Good gracious! Mr. Powers, what does this mean? What can it mean?"

"Deams, do you suppose that 'Henry Powers, Banker,' is going to take up with desk-room in this insignificant basement? Let me tell you I change my office to suit my position—"

"For mercy's sake, no joking. Let me know, truly, the meaning of all this."

"Come with me, Deams, and I will explain."

Deams followed me in silence.

I led the way to my new office, and unlocking the door, ushered him in.

"By Jove!" said Deams, brightening up; "I think I understand it now; Delain left his office to be let, I knew. I wonder I had not thought of it myself. You have got it at a bargain, I dare say. The rooms will suit us splendidly."

"*Me* you mean, Deams. I do not propose that any one shall occupy the place but myself."

"How so?" said Deams.

"Just this. I have undertaken, as you know, to float this new company. To do this, we must have separate offices."

"Do you really mean it?"

"Of course I do. Think a moment, Deams,"

I continued kindly, "and you will admit I am right; you yourself would not permit your name to be used on the prospectus, or as trustee, because you thought it would injure the Company. I appreciated your motives, and I want you to appreciate mine."

"I do, my dear Powers, I do," replied Deams, almost with tears in his eyes. "Your course is the correct one. It is better for you to have a respectable place to hail from, disconnected from mine. We can meet at my place when you like, and here when you like, while carrying out our plans."

"Exactly," I replied, and Deams left in excellent spirits.

I will let you, reader, a little further into my motives for so abruptly changing my place of business.

I had made a mistake in my connection with Deams, and determined in future to sail in company with the four first-class trustees, Messrs. Dempsey, Peters, Stillhouse, and Brokaw, and not with the members of the other department of the concern.

To do this I must cut loose from Deams, as well as from the associations of his office; and I must have a place where I should not be ashamed to ask my co-trustees to call on me.

I determined further, if any thing *should* go wrong in the affairs of the Company, that the four gentlemen I have mentioned should bear their full share of the responsibility.

Again, if I was to confer with Stokes, the large stock-broker, what could I expect hailing from that basement yonder?

You see I had calculated all the advantages before incurring this additional expense.

The next day I called on Mr. Stokes. He received me cordially, but was, of course, full of business. He proposed, however, to give me an interview at his house that evening, when I was to open up the subject of the "Hope and Anchor Mutual Coal Company."

Accordingly, about eight o'clock, I presented

myself at an elegant mansion in West Thirty-fourth Street.

I was ushered into a small library room, where I found Mr. Stokes comfortably smoking, while reading the *Evening Post*.

He welcomed me cordially, and offered me a cigar, which I accepted, and which proved to be of the choicest description.

After some general conversation about the war and the state of the country, I commenced my explanation. I went minutely into the matter, and explained the "situation," without reserve or keeping back. Finally I proposed to put the whole into the hands of his house, with such favorable arrangements as he himself should consider adequate for the services rendered.

"First, you want twelve thousand dollars to pay for the contract?"

"Yes."

"Then sixty thousand dollars for the first installment?"

"Yes."

"Then how much for opening and developing the mines, side tracks, cars, &c., &c., &c.?"

"A comparatively small sum would do at present," I replied, "besides the payments would be monthly."

"That makes little difference. We must count it as something to be raised now."

"Well, say fifty thousand dollars more."

"And the railroad through the property not yet finished?"

"Not quite. It will be in operation by the first of January. Quite as soon as we shall be able to avail ourselves of it."

"First of January means first of March or April," said Mr. Stokes.

"Possibly."

Thus far, the great broker had asked me questions with little or no comment. They were questions which I expected, and which were indeed not only proper but necessary. Still they produced the impression on me that

I should not succeed in my application, and what is more, that I ought not to succeed in it.

There was a considerable pause. It was broken by Mr. Stokes.

"Mr. Powers, let me say, in a word, that your enterprise is not yet in a condition for us to take hold of it.

"The fact is," he continued, "we have a good many constituents who depend very much on us in such an affair, and to whom we are in a measure morally responsible. You are not yet far enough along with the Company. Let me advise you to go to Dempsey and his friends, and let them advance the twelve thousand dollars and get rid of that contract. Or, what may perhaps be better for you, advance the money yourself. Then contrive some way to clear the land of any lien by mortgage, and you will have a 'case' we can act on. The stock is pretty severely 'watered,' but I don't mind that, if the property is *paid for*, so that stockholders really do own *something* when they hold shares."

"I was in hopes," I replied, "we might raise the twelve thousand and the sixty thousand through you. We can offer very great inducements. Indeed, I say frankly we expected to meet your views. We appreciate fully the advantages to come from your taking the matter up.

"Indeed," I continued, seeing Mr. Stokes remained provokingly silent, "excuse me for saying that I was induced to call on you from the few words you dropped the other day in the street."

"True, and I am glad you allude to it, for the circumstance had escaped my memory. You appear to me, sir," he continued, "to be straightforward and ingenuous. It is what I like. Let me tell you that open and plain dealing will help a man better in the 'street' than any circumlocution. I had heard of this enterprise, and knew several of the trustees. I was told further that

Mr. Worth was to be included in it. If it had been launched with no debt, as I supposed it would be, I was ready to take it up—not otherwise."

I began gradually to gather a better impression of Wall Street men. "Not quite so unscrupulous," I said to myself, "as I have been led to believe. At least, it seems there are some things they are not willing to do, even to make money."

I know what Deams would have said—namely: "Stokes has too much at stake to risk his reputation in taking up a doubtful enterprise,—that is why he declines."

I sat quite silent for a moment or two, while Mr. Stokes continued at his cigar. At length I asked him if he could recommend any house to me, who would be likely to take the affair up.

"I do not think any first-class house will do it; and certainly, with those names, you do not want to expose the affair to second-rate people.

Follow my advice, Mr. Powers. Take your time, and get the whole affair well into shape. The property is very large, and the reports are good, and, as I have said, it will bear diluting. In the mean time, keep it clean—let none of the stock get out, and when you are all right come to me. I will put it on the board, and it shall go! But not as it is now, not in its present shape. Glad to see you here. Take another cigar as you go out. Stay, a glass of sherry? No? Good evening."

Here was my first failure. Never mind, I soliloquized, I have learned something at all events. I think better of Stokes than I did before I called on him. If he is not more honest, he is, at least, more wise than many of his confreres.

Notwithstanding my encomiums on the great broker, I felt sorely disappointed at the result of my interview, and walked slowly homeward, in no enviable state of mind.

At my age rebuffs were disheartening, especially when they came from a respectable quarter. I had not then learned their value in giving the character strength by producing a fresh resistance and energy.

CHAPTER XXIV.

"I WILL put it through, though," were the first words I uttered to myself the next morning on waking. "I WILL put it through."

Excited by the intensity of my resolution, I dressed rapidly, swallowed my coffee and toast in haste, and proceeded down town with a conscience less scrupulous than on the previous day.

Mark the confession.

There are various ways by which men lapse slowly, but surely, until they descend quite to the standard of knaves. Many are the avenues sloping gracefully downward to——

Stay, I did not undertake to write a book of moralizing. I am to record simply some facts, yes, facts within my own experience, and you, reader, must educe the moral, which always accompanies truth.

I am no hero, no saint, no villain; but simply a successful "Wall Street" man; successful, perhaps, where many would have failed; how, and by what means successful, I am about to tell you, without comment of my own.

In future, then, if I proceed to record what strikes you as not quite up to the standard of common honesty, you need not infer any approval from my silence, any more than you would take it for granted I condemn a good action because I fail to applaud it.

With this understanding, let us proceed.

I confess I did not feel quite ready to encounter Deams that day. I knew he had an extravagant faith in what I could accomplish, and I was sorry to meet him while still somewhat diminished in my own regard.

However, I got along with the interview without permitting my "ancient" to lose confidence in his chief.

I remarked to Deams that "it was in train;" the matter was looking as "favorable as I could
11

expect," (!) and I should report as soon as I required his services.

"What a fool I am," I said, after Deams had left the office, "what a fool I am. Why should I assume the whole burden, when we have men of wealth and influence in our board? I will call on these gentlemen, and they shall aid me to float the Company. They must each *do* something toward earning their ten thousand dollars of stock."

Inspired by this new thought, I went to the office of the Antarctic Iron Mills, of which large and lucrative concern Mr. Dempsey was the head.

I found him very busy, and it was with difficulty, after waiting half an hour, I could get an interview. At length, however, I took advantage of a favorable opportunity to say I wished a few moments' conversation with him.

Mr. Dempsey received me very kindly. I found him amiable in his general demeanor, and the tone in which he requested me to be seated, impressed me so favorably that I felt assured that

I had only to state the case, in order to receive his hearty support and co-operation.

"I called on you to confer about the Hope and Anchor Mutual Coal Company," I said. "My name is Powers. I am one of the trustees. I——"

"Oh, Mr. Powers, Mr. Henry Powers," interrupted Mr. Dempsey, "you are an acquaintance of my good friend Mr. Pope. A most worthy person, a good man, a really good man. He is indefatigable in our church, zealous in good works. Yes, he gives you a high character, I must say, a very high character."

I bowed in acknowledgment of the statement. The announcement that I was indebted to the little man with the carroty wig and goggle eyes for the kind appreciation of Mr. Dempsey, was not altogether to my taste.

"Any one coming with a recommendation from Mr. Pope," continued Mr. Dempsey, "is entitled to a hearing, no matter how much engaged I am. I hope the Company is well under way. Have you any coal in yet? I was told by a

Mr.—ahem! Mr.—Mr. Leams, I think was his name—you must know him, by the way—your shipping agent at Shawnee, that coal would be received by the Company in the course of the month, and it is now the 25th.

"Let me see," he proceeded, without waiting for any reply, "let me see, I have already several orders—a blessed thing to serve the poor—here they are. I was going to send them down to Mr. Pope, perhaps you will do me the favor to take them.

"Here is 'half a ton to No. 390 East Street;' 'one ton No. 211 same Street;' 'half ton No. 70 Early Street;' all these I will pay for at cost price on presentation of receipt by carman.

"By the way, I told Mr. Pope I should advise *not* to charge any cartage to the poor. Having so many in your employ the Company won't feel it, and the poor will, don't you think so?"

I bowed again. I saw I was in deep water; that is, utterly ignorant of what had been said to Mr. Dempsey, to induce him to become

President, although Deams had professed to en-
lighten me.

I say " in deep water," for I began much to
fear if I put the matter before him as I had proposed, Mr. Dempsey would immediately resign,
and thereupon would follow an entire break-up of
the whole concern; all caused by my own imprudence.

There was a brief pause, which I improved by
reaching my hand for the valuable coal orders,
and by bowing again. I could think of nothing
I dared *say*.

" So you are delivering already? Well, that
is making good time," continued Mr. Dempsey.

" We are in hopes you will look in daily at
the Company's offices," I said, perceiving he
waited for an answer, which I determined not to
give. " You pass them twice a day, and your
presence, even for a moment, will help to give
encouragement to our plans."

" Oh, your plan is a good one, a good one,
really and truly. I am satisfied of it, or, you

know, I could not consent to the use of my
name. Beyond that, I am perfectly positive Mr.
Pope would permit nothing which is not honest.
Besides, he speaks well of you, too, and you
appear to be an active man.

"I told Mr. Pope I would come whenever any
thing was actually necessary to be passed on by
the board; that will be seldom, you know; the
finance committee, of which Mr. Pope and yourself make two out of three, have full powers.
You see I have looked carefully into it."

This was news to me. It turned out the cunning Deams had had the meeting for organization
before consulting me at all; had passed by-laws
ready made, appointed committees, and generally
got ready for action, intending, as he really did,
to insure my co-operation afterward.

What should I do? Attempt to back gracefully out of the interview, content with doing the
Company no damage, or should I try gently to
accomplish something.

I decided on the latter course.

"Mr. Dempsey, we have, as you know, a little matter of twelve thousand dollars to raise, and I thought it would be best for a few of us to put our hands in our pockets and make a finish of it. I will be one of four or five to do so," I continued, stoutly.

"I think you had better not push this, Mr. Powers; the fact is, my son-in-law did not like the idea of going into the board, and, indeed, objected to my taking the position of President. Our friends, Peters and Brokaw, did not come in very willingly either; and it was distinctly understood that none of them should be called on for money.

"I fear, if you should put the matter before them, they would resign, and that wouldn't do; that wouldn't do, would it?

"I talk to you frankly," continued Mr. Dempsey, after a pause, "because Mr. Pope gives you such an excellent character; and, in fact, I like your face. You look to me like an honest young man!"

"*An honest young man!*" The words smote my very soul. I turned red.

"Do not be discouraged," said Mr. Dempsey, kindly, "but keep on the way you have begun, and the Company will soon be in an easy condition. Why don't you just advance the twelve thousand dollars yourself? You are a banker, I am told; advance it yourself. I dare say the next ninety days will see you reimbursed. Come, now, that is not a bad suggestion, is it?"

Mr. Dempsey smiled pleasantly.

I, too, smiled, but with a contortion of spirit badly concealed, I fear, by the outward expression.

It is not to be supposed that I committed myself to the suggestion of the worthy President; at the same time, I did not tell him that it was impracticable. On the contrary, as I rose to take leave of him, I said I would "see what could be done."

"Of course you will," said Mr. Dempsey, grasping my hand warmly, "and it will all come

right too. I see it in your eye. Yes, indeed!
Good day, good day. Drop in whenever you
can, and—don't forget those little orders; the
weather is getting cold, and the poor suffer—they
suffer, you know, when frost comes."

I know *I* "suffered," as I quitted the place of
that kind and simple-hearted good man.

As I walked up the street my breast was
filled with conflicting emotions. I was half inclined to go back, request a private interview,
give Mr. Dempsey a brief history of my career,
expose the bubble of the Coal Company, and ask
him to give me a place in his concern, where I
could make myself useful, and gradually work up
to a superior position.

"I shall have peace of mind at least," I said
to myself; "and——"

"Hallo! what are you doing in this quarter?"

It was the voice of a Wall Street acquaintance, a young man of wealth and position, and
prominent in affairs.

He was standing directly opposite; but I
11*

had not noticed it in my abstracted state of mind.

"What are you doing here yourself?" I replied, adapting my own manner to his.

"I am going to the office of the Antarctic Works, to see about an order for iron that we are to advance on when delivered," he replied, crossing over and shaking hands with me at the same time.

"By the way, I think I may guess where you have been. Dempsey is President of your Coal Company, I see. You could not have a better man. I received your prospectus this morning. It looks first-rate. I guess you have got a good thing there. Good day!"

Here it was again! One revulsion succeeds another. The words of my acquaintance had an intoxicating effect on me.

My *other* angel whispered, "Powers, you will learn by and by not to be chicken-hearted. Everybody thinks well of this scheme. Why not think well of it yourself? As to these four eminent gentlemen who have consented to act as trustees, why, let them alone, and 'bank' all you can on their reputation. Meantime, courage, keep trying and the right man will be found."

.　　.　　.　　.　　.　　.　　.

I walked on to Deams's office. He rose as I entered, as if expecting to hear some very good news.

"I have been to see Mr. Dempsey," I said.

"Good gracious!" exclaimed Deams, sinking suddenly back in his chair, as if prostrated by the intelligence. "How *could* you commit such an imprudence?"

"What do you mean?"

"My dear Powers, you should not have gone near him without consulting me."

"I discovered as much very soon. In one word, there is no harm done. I did not come to talk about that."

"Well?"

"Deams?"

"What is it?"

"We must commence delivering coal to-morrow, according to our prospectus."

"Bah, don't be so facetious."

"I am not joking, I am only carrying out the promise made by our *shipping agent* at Shawnee."

"Now don't be severe on me, Powers. I had to make the promise. Old Dempsey pushed me so hard I could not help it."

"It is quite right," I said, "just right. Do you go at once to Essex and Lee—they are the largest coal-dealers in the city—and make an arrangement with them to fill any orders that may come in, and charge us the wholesale price. I have no doubt this can be done so that we shall not lose more than fifty cents a ton, and that we must manage to stand somehow."

"Take my hat," said Deams in great glee. "You are worthy of it. That is a brilliant stroke of policy, and no mistake. I wonder I had not thought of it.

"I will fix the matter to-day," continued

Deams, energetically, "and report to our President to-morrow."

"The sooner the better, Deams."

CHAPTER XXV.

THE advertisement that the Hope and Anchor Mutual Coal Company were ready to deliver coal to the shareholders at cost, created considerable excitement among boarding-house keepers and economical family men. A score of melancholy-eyed women presented themselves at the attract-ive counter of Masterman, Coldbrook & Pope, each eager to secure a winter supply of coal for her establishment.

Small men with large families crowded the passage-way, all anxious for coal at cost.

Somehow most of them were under the impression that it was sufficient to be a stock-holder—that is, the owner of one share, price five dollars—to enable them to receive all the coal they should desire; and they were greatly dis-gusted when informed by little Mr, Pope that they could have one ton at cost only for every share of stock subscribed and paid for.

Meanwhile, the advertisements were continued in the daily papers, attracting much attention.

Leaving to Masterman, Coldbrook & Pope the management of the various applicants for coal at cost, and to Deams the delivery of coal to the poor (an extraordinary employment that for Deams), I bent all my energies to the task of securing some one to take up our Company.

Day after day went by and found me no nearer my object. I had applied to two or three different brokers of the first class, but without success. Stokes was right when he told me I would find no such men to undertake it as it then stood.

It is true I did not commit myself to explanations as fully as I had to him. I had grown more wary and discriminating; but I said enough, and ascertained enough, to be satisfied my case was hopeless.

I think at this time I should have abandoned

the scheme, so weary was I with it and with its repulsive surroundings, had I not overtaken Mary Worth one day as I was walking homeward.

I slackened my pace as I came up, irresistibly impelled to do so by the desire to linger near her.

She was in company with a gentleman, a rich young New-York blood, who had nothing to do but to dress and drive, and be agreeable to the ladies.

I had frequently heard Bellamy's name in connection with Miss Worth's as her admirer, if not her accepted suitor. I did not credit the reports, for, with all my doubts and fears, I could not make myself believe he was at all to her taste.

A pang of jealousy, notwithstanding, darted through me as I saw the two sauntering leisurely along the grand promenade that fine October afternoon; *he* all gallantry and devotion, *she* receiving his attentions as it seemed to me, with an interested air.

I thought at first I would pass rapidly along without appearing to notice her; but I was ashamed of such weakness, and as we met, I turned and saluted her with politeness but with my accustomed formality.

Could I be mistaken? Was the wish father to the thought? It seemed, positively it seemed, as her eyes fell upon me, that she perceived my pained look (for I could not have concealed it), and cast on me a glance, which said, as I thought, " you need not feel alarmed, I am merely amusing myself. I don't care for him a bit."

Perhaps it was in my imagination, but it sent the blood dancing through my veins.

I went into a shop and purchased some trifling article, so as to give them an opportunity to go by me. I confess it. I wished to take another look at Mary Worth.

I stopped and gazed after her. I looked at the miserable fop—so I was ready to call him—who was walking at her side. What right had such a jackanapes to be rolling in wealth, and enjoying all that is desirable on this earth, while I, his superior every way, was slaving on in this degrading manner?

With clinched hands and set teeth I pursued my way.

The next morning brought a new plan and a new party to light.

CHAPTER XXVI.

Just around the corner of Wall Street, in William, near Exchange Place, is a large building filled with offices.

These rooms are occupied by brokers, money-lenders, railroad companies, speculators, and lawyers.

It would be curious if, Asmodeus-like, we could take off the roofs that cover the heads of all the different occupants of this same building, and witness the busy workings of their brain. It would present a strange mixture, interesting to the student and the philosopher, but conveying no very new impression to the denizen of the "Street," who is already entirely familiar with the subject in every possible phase.

There is a small room in this building-furnished with a plain pine table, a large and expensive safe of the best make, an arm-chair, and an old sofa.

A small tin sign, on which is painted " J. STYKES," announces correctly the name of the tenant.

Every one knows John Stykes, so it is scarcely necessary for me to describe him. However, for the benefit of those who do not reside in New York, I will say that he is a man a little past middle age, with delicately curved features, a finely chiseled Roman nose, large gray eyes, and pale face, almost approaching the cadaverous. His hair is jet black, his height medium, his person slender.

A remarkable man in appearance; indeed, you would say an interesting one. There is nothing disagreeable in his manner or conversation. He is well-educated and well-informed; and with his family goes into the best society, where he spends money without stint.

In a sense, this man is trustworthy, never breaking a promise, and always living up to his agreement. But he is unscrupulous in carrying out his plans, and ready and quick to take advantage of the weakness of another's position. Exorbitant in his claims, he is pitiless and remorseless to any one in his power.

Exacting, unrelenting, cold, he sits and takes in, not with his ear, as it would seem, but rather with his large serpent eye, all that you say to him. Then he replies quietly and in measured tones, and from what he says you need make no appeal.

This man deals in money, and in operations which require the *immediate* use of money. As I have described him as he is now, so he was at the time of my engaging in the Hope and Anchor Company.

To this man I resolved to go!

I had seen him two or three times, in the office of an intimate acquaintance, and was, to an extent, fascinated by his peculiar appearance and conversation.

I soon gathered the particulars which I have

given to the reader, and which no one will venture to contradict.

I met Mr. Stykes once shortly after my return from Long Branch.

He came into the place where I was taking lunch with a friend. Two or three were speaking of my adventure, and passed many encomiums on what they were pleased to call my heroism.

Just then I happened to raise my eyes and encountered those of Stykes, who had entered quietly, and was a silent listener to the conversation.

I can scarcely say why, but it sent a chill through me to look at him. If any expression could be gained from his countenance, it was one of subdued contempt.

The moment he saw I was looking at him, however, he changed his position, and asked in an indifferent tone: "Did you know whom you were rescuing?"

"No," I replied.

"Indeed," he said, and the subject was dropped.

.   .   .   .

In accordance with my resolution, I called on Mr. Stykes. I found him in his office alone, carefully scrutinizing a document which he held in his hand.

He looked up as I entered, and nodded to me in token of recognition.

"Mr. Stykes," I. said, "I want a half-hour's conversation with you."

"On what subject?"

"About the Hope and Anchor Mutual Coal Company."

"I don't advance money to new companies."

"I know it. I don't want you to advance money. I want a half-hour's talk with you. You can probably tell in five minutes whether you wish me to proceed or not."

"Are you an early man?"

"Yes."

"Call in to-morrow morning at nine o'clock."

"Good-day."

Mr. Stykes vouchsafed no response to my parting salutation. I was content, however.

The rest of the day I devoted to a careful consideration of the position I was in, and of how best to approach the subtle man of money.

As the result of my cogitations, I had to admit to myself, that in the combat of wits which was to come off, Mr. Stykes had the advantage every way. He was older, richer, more cunning, and more unscrupulous than I. Besides, I was the seeker, not he.

What should I do? How should I manage? That was the question.

On due deliberation I resolved not to manage at all, but tell Stykes the whole story and give him at the start the making of the terms which in the end he was sure to dictate.

Precisely at nine o'clock I was at his office.

Not to tire the reader with repetition, I will only say that I gave Mr. Stykes a minute and faithful account of the Hope and Anchor enterprise; so minute and faithful that, when I had concluded, he knew as much about it as I did.

I wound up as follows: "Now, Mr. Stykes, are you willing to take the thing up, and on what terms?"

During the recital, Mr. Stykes' large stone eyes were slowly rolling so as to take in my whole person, my face being his central point. In spite of me, it seemed as if I were undergoing a certain anaconda process preparatory to being swallowed whole, along with my Coal Company.

"You think the coal is there?" said Mr. Stykes after a long silence.

"Yes."

"It probably *is* there," he continued, as if thinking aloud, "the Shawnee region is a good one."

Another long pause, which I did not interrupt.

12

At length Mr. Stykes spoke. "I will do this," he said.

"In the first place I must be satisfied about the property. The reports of Quartz and Silex I would not give a fig for. They are eminent, scientific men; but I can buy a report from every scientific man in America for a thousand dollars a piece.

"I say I will do this; I will take my own lawyer and my own miner, and visit the property; if I am satisfied with it, I will pay the twelve thousand dollars you are in such want of, and set the Company in motion. The stock shall *all* be placed in my hands, and put under my lock and key. I shall operate with it just as I please. In fact, control it entirely. Two hundred thousand dollars of it shall be transferred to some one I shall indicate for my own account. The Company's shares I shall have the right to operate with, holding myself responsible to the Company for the stock or its proceeds. The cash payments you and your friends must waive.

I shall doubtless be obliged to advance the sixty thousand dollars, and take a mortgage on the property from the Company. The present Board must hold their places. I will pay the expenses of the office—that is, rent, clerk-hire, and petty incidentals; and will take the furniture at a valuation, if you desire.

"Further," continued Mr. Stykes, as he permitted his eye to *settle* on me, while it assumed, I will not say a softer, but a less hard expression,—"further, a thousand dollars cash for yourself, for your agency in the matter.

"Think this over," said Mr. Stykes, rising as if to put an end to further conversation," and let me have your decision at this hour to-morrow."

I went out from the presence of the man, feeling quite satisfied that the process had been thoroughly completed with me, I couldn't precisely explain how. I felt assured that all chance of realizing beyond exactly what he promised would terminate on the acceptance of his proposition.

I proceeded immediately to Deams's office.

"It is all up with us," I said.

Deams was in great terror.

"I have done my best, Deams, and I can not float the Company."

"What is the matter? What has happened?"

"Nothing at all, except that I am unable to carry out the scheme; but I tell you what I can do, Deams; I can sell out to John Stykes and get the twelve thousand dollars, and a thousand dollars besides for ourselves."

"Magnificent! Splendid!" cried Deams. "What did you want to frighten me so, for? So Stykes is to take it. What is to become of all our stock?"

"We hold it the same as under the old plan, but it is to be all under lock and key till money is raised for the Company."

"Why that's honest; that's right," said Deams, "that's the way it should be. If Stykes takes hold of it, it will go, and our shares will be worth par in time. How about the yearly payments after the first sixty thousand?"

"Wiped out."

"I thought as much," said Deams, "I only put it in as a flyer. Powers, I always said you were a trump, and you have proved it. It is not everybody that could have got hold of John Stykes as you have——"

"I thought when I was with him that he had got hold of me."

Deams laughed. "You are a good deal of a wag. Come, let us have lunch. I think I can go a bottle of champagne on this morning's news. We will take it quietly over at Hinkley's, and you can then go into particulars."

It is only necessary for me to observe that Deams was more than satisfied with the result of my efforts. Cash in hand was all he wanted —much or little, and the sum he was to receive was quite unprecedented in his later experience.

From some expressions which fell from him, I was satisfied he had had very little confidence in the affair, and that he really regarded it as a passing scheme to raise the wind. However, I forgave him for attempting to play on my credulity, since he did not succeed, at least to any extent.

On separating, I extorted a promise that he would scrupulously follow my directions in every thing relating to the Company. I told him not to count his chickens before they were hatched, since all depended on Stykes' personal examination of the property; and meantime he must be careful not to speak to any one on the subject.

I did not close my eyes that night.

It seemed as if I had made, as it were, providentially, a great escape. I could now see clearly on what a frail basis I was about to risk all that I had, namely, my reputation. Yes, reputation was after all dear to me, when it came to the test. More dear to me, perhaps, because if not established, it was not as yet tarnished.

.   .   .   .

"What if the property is not satisfactory? What if the titles prove defective?"

The very thought made me hold my breath. "I will not indulge in forebodings. I will accept Mr. Stykes' proposition at nine o'clock tomorrow morning sharp, and leave the future to my good angel—Mary Worth!"

CHAPTER XXVII.

THE next day, and punctual ·to the moment, I was at Mr. Stykes' little office in William Street.

He was deeply occupied as usual, but laid aside his papers as I entered, and waited for me to announce my acceptance or refusal of his offer.

"Mr. Stykes," I said, "I accede to the terms you offer, with one very slight exception."

"What is it?"

"You stipulate to have the board remain as it is. I agree, mainly, to that. I am a member. My name brings no sort of influence with it, as you know. I must insist on withdrawing it. You may put a man of your own choosing in my place."

Mr. Stykes looked me steadily in the face,

his eye, always slowly moving, yet firm on its axis.

I returned his look with one sharp and decisive.

For an instant Mr. Stykes permitted a ray of appreciative intelligence to escape him; the next moment he had settled again into his natural appalling indifference.

"As you like," he replied, "it is a matter of no consequence to me."

"When will you have finished your examination?" I asked.

"In a week."

"You will then be ready to conclude the arrangements?"

"If all things prove satisfactory, yes."

.   .   .   .

I had great difficulty during those seven days in restraining Deams. In spite of his promise to me, he was constantly on the point of betraying that something immensely important

12*

was about to happen. The pompous airs he assumed, the petty debts he incurred, and the lofty contempt for trifles he exhibited, were very ludicrous.

At length the day arrived when I was to receive Mr. Stykes' answer.

I confess it was not without a degree of trepidation that I mounted the stairs, and entered his room.

My pulse beat fast as I said, " Good morning." It was in a rapid manner—too rapid and off guard as I now recollect, that I enunciated, —" I have called to learn the result of your investigation."

" It is satisfactory. Sit down. I have prepared a memorandum of what I wish done for your own government, and which comes within the scope of my offer. Let all the papers be sent to Izzy, Quincy Court; he will prepare what I wish signed. Then let your people make the transfer of the contract to the Company, and the twelve thousand dollars are ready.

"I will take the Company's obligation for that amount, payable from the first receipts of sale of the Company's shares.

"I shall communicate with you only.

"Let the board be called together, and make your own explanations in your own way, but carry out *this* (putting his finger on the paper) in every particular. When you are ready, I am."

"Who do you propose shall take my place at the board?"

"You will not remain?"

"No."

"You may serve your own interests by staying in."

"I have decided to resign."

Mr. Stykes took a narrow slip of paper, wrote the name of an individual I never heard of, and added his address, which was in a fashionable quarter of the city, and handed me the slip.

"Not in business?" I said.

"No! retired."

.   .   .   .

I need not tell you, reader, that I set my-self with energy to the work of carrying out the programme which Mr. Stykes had pre-pared.

I could not but notice it was strictly in accordance with the terms verbally expressed to me.

To Deams I left the labor of explanation.

I never inquired, and I never permitted him to tell me what representations he made, what arguments he used, or what inducements he held out.

Suffice it to say, all went smoothly at the "Board." I resigned, and "Elias Ashley" was unanimously chosen in my place.

As I left the room, Mr. Dempsey shook me cordially by the hand.

"We dislike much to part with you," he said, "but we quite understand how you can be of more service to us in your new career, if you are not a member of our board."

IIis words were "Greek" to me. I did not comprehend what he meant, and have never discovered since.

I said not one word in reply. I only smiled, and bowing my adieu, I left the office of the IIope and Anchor Mutual Coal Company forever.

Of the twelve thousand dollars, the share of Deams and myself was three thousand—fifteen hundred dollars apiece. The thousand dollars which I had from Stykes, I divided with Deams, and received from him two hundred and fifty dollars so long due, and immediately paid my debt to my friend IIolman.

Next I removed my quarters from the moderate boarding-house I was living at to the sixth story of the Grand Avenue Hotel.

This was from no sudden impulse or foolish regard for appearances.

I was determined to change all my associations, and in future frequent the society of people who had money, and avoid all poor devils, at least, till I was in a situation to afford to keep company with them, should I desire to do so.

For the rest I was careful and economical in my habits, and resolved that the inroads on my two thousand dollars should be as light and infrequent as possible.

I was fully determined before this sum should be expended, to find my way into some respectable occupation, or quit the city.

CHAPTER XXVIII.

Although forming no part of my personal history or experience, you may very naturally desire to know what became of the well-known Coal Company which I have heretofore introduced to you.

Your reasonable curiosity shall be gratified.

You will please bear in mind that the actual sum to be paid the proprietor, Grover P. Wilcox, for the coal lands, was sixty thousand dollars.

The price was really very low, but the terms were imperative—*cash.*

In vain Deams had attempted to procure a credit of one year.

Therefore, so long as the sixty thousand remained unpaid, the Company could receive no deed, and had, literally, nothing to rest upon.

The first thing which was done under the

Stykes administration (not that he ever appeared in any thing which was going forward), was the execution of a mortgage by the Company to this same Grover P. Wilcox, for the sixty thousand dollars, payable in six months.

This mortgage was taken to Mr. Wilcox, and along with it the money for the lands, with the request that he would convey the lands to the Company, and transfer the mortgage to John Stykes of the City of New York.

This was all very natural and proper, and Mr. Wilcox complied.

Then began the great season of prosperity for the "Hope and Anchor!"

Gradually it found its way, as it would seem, by sheer force of merit on the stock list. A transfer-clerk was added to the establishment— one of Stykes's appointing.

That gentleman having purchased the furniture which adorned the offices of Masterman, Coldbrook & Pope, and taken the assignment of their lease, intimated in due time to them by one of his mysterious agents (as I have said he never acted in person), that the Coal Company would require all the room for its legitimate business, and it would be advisable for them to remove their "banking-house" to another quarter.

Mr. Stykes, however, insisted on their remaining in the board. Indeed he could not dispense with Mr. Pope's services as secretary, only he proposed to hire a competent young man to do the drudgery of writing up the records, preparing new certificates, and so forth.

Mr. Masterman was inclined to resist—the idea of *his* resisting John Stykes!

On this occasion his friend Deams did not stand by him. On the contrary, after some hot words, Deams told him he had been very well paid for his services, and, indeed, more than paid, that he very well knew it, and he need not attempt to humbug him—the virtuous Deams!

Masterman left the premises in a huff, and immediately resigned his office as treasurer. It was filled by Elias Ashley.

Mr. Pope, on his part, was delighted. Neither he nor Coldbrook ever relished their new position, or the honors attending it. Besides, it really interfered with their business, which they were tempted to neglect.

They had now got well out of the furniture question, and had made a little ready money, and they had no wish to prolong their connection with Masterman. So the eminent and highly respectable "banking-house" went into liquidation.

It owed nothing—Masterman had tried in vain to run in debt on its reputation—and it consequently had to pay nothing.

Messrs. Pope and Coldbrook returned to their respective employments, content in the future to labor there. Mr. Pope, however, called daily at the office of the "Hope and Anchor" (he was under a small salary), to sign his name as secretary to whatever was necessary.

This was to propitiate ·Mr. Dempsey, for so long as *he* was content, his friends in the board naturally would remain so,

At length, "Hope and Anchor" became active. It was noticed regularly in the money articles of the daily papers, and occasionally would appear an additional line in recommendation of the "Mutual plan."

But nothing like a "puff" was anywhere permitted. All was dignified and decorous, and very much above board.

Finally, the *Independent* took the Company up, and its triumph was complete.

It was a very cold winter, and through the whole of it, the request of any respectable citizen for delivery of small quantities of coal to any poor person at cost, was promptly complied with.

I do not think, however, there were many subscriptions for shares received at the office. People were referred to Eppis, Ippis, and Oppis (the largest stock-brokers in the Street, as everybody knows), who now had entire charge of the Company's operations.

It was curious to witness the fluctuations in

this famous stock, and how it went up and how
it went down, and how it went up again.

There were rumors of a corner, and everybody
stood from under. The gate was opened again,
and everybody rushed in. Indeed, "Hope and
Anchor" was in every one's mouth. It was the
talk of the clubs, and the main topic of conversation in the *salons* It was even dealt in during
the evening in the hall of the Grand Avenue
Hotel.

Never was there such a favorite stock with
the brokers.

Meantime, Mr. Stykes made regular formal reports of his operations to the Company. Now the
twelve thousand dollars had been repaid to him.

That was well.

Next came the construction account. No
money must be spared to put the property in
good working condition, and at once.

All agreed to that.

At the end of the year, another report set
forth that at least a hundred thousand dollars

had been expended, and well expended in developing the mine, which sum had been realized by sale of the Company's shares at par.

This was certainly very promising; what could be more promising?

Meanwhile, mark you, the *mortgage* for sixty thousand dollars stood against the property and improvements, and that mortgage was owned by John Stykes.

Affairs went on very prosperously through the winter and spring.

As summer approached, and the dull season began, there suddenly came a contraction in the money market

Along with this were painful rumors about the "Hope and Anchor."

Some said the Company had a large mortgage debt, which was now pressing against it; others, that it had foolishly indulged in speculation in its own stock; others hinted at an over-issue, while others still declared they never had had any confidence in it whatever!

Down went the shares.

Down went Jones, and Robinson, and Smith, and Thompson, and Brown, and Green, who had each embarked his little shallop on the apparently smooth sea of the " Hope and Anchor."

" Why don't some one call a meeting of the creditors," said Jones, "and show up the rascally swindle !"

Alas, there *were* no creditors. John Stykes was too shrewd an operator for that.

But the stockholders? Why not call an indignation meeting of the stockholders?" said Robinson, in a despairing tone.

Everybody in the Street smiled when Robinson said this, and asked him how many shares he had.—He had just fifty at five dollars !

In fact there was not so very much stock afloat after all. Stykes had quietly purchased in the most of it when it fell to fifty cents a share.

So the " Street " only laughed and called it cleverly done, and then turned their attention to the next new " fancy."

The mortgage against the Company was duly "foreclosed," and John Stykes became the owner of the fine property, now ready, really ready for working.

He had paid for the whole out of his manipulations of the shares, and cleared a large sum besides.

The Company closed its doors.

None of the four influential directors had lost any thing; not even reputation, for their characters for honesty were too firmly established for them to suffer in that respect.

In due time a solid company was established to mine these very coal lands. Stykes holds a majority of the stock. It is actually worth to-day—shares one hundred dollars—one hundred and twenty. On "freezing out" the original parties, this is the satisfactory result.

After all it was nothing but a Wall Street encounter of wits. The public did not suffer— much. And the succeeding winter many a poor wretch tried in vain to find the office of that charitable company who gave them coal at cost!

They bless the name of the "HOPE AND ANCHOR" to this day!

CHAPTER XXIX.

It is a terrible thing for a man who is active, energetic, and fresh, to be landed high and dry upon a sand-bank.

The proximity to the water, where he sees vessels under full sail, only aggravates his condition.

How to get off? That is the question.

That was *my* question for a long time after retiring from the enterprise I had so rashly undertaken, but from which I had certainly got well away.

Once more unshackled, with the additional advantage that I was in no immediate pecuniary want, I took a cool, calculating view of the business life with which I was surrounded, and in which the quickest, keenest intellects of the world encounter each other.

13

"A man who owes nothing, and has three cents over, can pass for a millionaire."

This apothegm of Deams I now took full advantage of: not for the purpose of obtaining any thing from the public under false pretenses, unless it might be the public's favorable opinion. That, however, I felt myself entitled to until I had done something to forfeit it.

I continued my residence at the Grand Avenue Hotel, and paid my bills with the quiet air of a solid man. I went regularly to my office, from whence I regarded with attention the course of affairs.

The money-market, stock list, fluctuations in gold, exchange, provisions, dry-goods, were all watched with the closest scrutiny.

In short, I put myself to school. I sought acquaintance with the "best" men, and asked for opinions and judgments with the tone of a person who has his own views, and who can therefore afford to inquire into theirs. Above all, I kept my own counsel.

It was not long before I heard myself spoken of as "a young man of great sagacity." "Very careful operator," another remarked. "Silent and shrewd," quoth a third.

Men of influence in the "Street," now bowed to me with a certain. degree of consideration, and propositions were made from time to time which, if I had had the means to accept, would have been extremely desirable. These, of course, I found a way for declining without betraying the secret of my situation.

Other schemes purely speculative, I dismissed summarily, giving those who presented them to understand that I "never touched any thing of the sort."

It was in vain the poor fellows sought to modify my judgment. I was inexorable!

At times it made my heart ache to see some one who *put me in mind of myself.* On two or three occasions I remember to have advised young men, who appeared to be still fresh and un-hackneyed, to quit the city, and the invariable response was, "we have not the means to do it."

I should say something here of the very satisfactory conduct of Deams.

That extraordinary individual still continued to haunt the purlieus of the stock board, maintaining his old character and habits. Although he never approached me with any more "enterprises," he was always not only cordial, but, I was about to say, affectionate in his manner. Wherever he went he spoke of me as "an extraordinary man," "one of the most successful men in the Street," and the like.

Mr. Worth was now in the habit of stopping me occasionally to ask some financial question, which he supposed my own affairs made me familiar with, but which only the most careful study of, and attention to business matters made it possible for me to reply to.

Even John Stykes did not omit to nod as we encountered each other! At church, the leading members of the congregation began to notice me.

By degrees I was proffered introductions to the young ladies. Matters were moving on charmingly.

Only I was all this time high and dry on the sand bank I spoke of at the commencement of the chapter.

I knew it, if no one else did. I knew it, and at times smiled grimly when I thought of my position—smiled grimly at the attention I received from " sound business - men "—grimly when I perceived young ladies seeking an introduction.

But I never so smiled when Mary Worth was near. My manner toward her was always the same. It was always, as at the first, entirely natural, though perhaps formal, showing a sincere respect and regard.

I did not seek a more intimate acquaintance with her, because things *appeared* so bright with me. I had no objection to availing myself of the attentions which were generally bestowed on me. The politeness of our church-

going people was as fully understood and appreciated as their neglect had been, and I felt
quite at liberty to take advantage of it.

To Mary Worth I could present no false
token. She must have thought it singular, understanding, as I am sure she did, why I had
not pressed my acquaintance, and having every
reason to suppose that the objection I had myself interposed no longer existed.

I could not help it. I must not betray my
secret; so I kept on the even tenor of my
way.

Occasionally I detected her looking at me
with a half-curious, half-troubled expression which
I did not quite understand. Her influence over
me increased all the while, until I felt a strong
mysterious conviction that her destiny was to
be blended with mine. A strange state of
things—yet there it was! "She is mine, she
can not escape me, mine forever," I would exclaim, as if inspired by some divinity!

CHAPTER XXX.

During the winter I received many invitations to parties, receptions, private theatricals, etc., etc.

These were proffered because it was understood I was a very prosperous young man, who bid fair to make his mark in the financial world. This was all that the various papas and mammas seemed to care for or even think of, and, I may add, the daughters also.

I accepted a great many of these invitations for the simple purpose of mixing socially in fashionable society, and seeing what it was made of.

I confess I found it very pleasant indeed. I took pleasure in looking at the handsome women, dressed expensively and in good taste, who governed themselves by certain rules of etiquette, which excluded vulgarity and made every thing agreeable.

I did not attempt to penetrate below the surface, but took things as they appeared.

In this way I enjoyed myself exceedingly.

At many of these parties I saw Miss Worth.

Here was an opportunity for meeting her not only on neutral ground, but on equal ground, where, surrounded by so much that made the scene romantic and fairy-like, I might renew the intimacy which we had at the sea-shore.

I was sorely tempted. But the recollection of the conversation I overheard at Long Branch, and the look of anxiety worn by Mr. Worth at that time, still haunted me, still stirred my pride.

I never omitted, however, to speak to Miss Worth whenever I did meet her in society, yet I carefully abstained from any further attentions. But I never devoted myself for the evening, after the fashion of many young men, to any one of the young ladies of my acquaintances. I endeavored to be polite without being demonstrative.

One evening, however, at a magnificent party given by Mrs. De Castro, I found myself after dancing with a very charming girl, Miss Edgerton, daughter of a wealthy New Yorker, seated near a window, in conversation with her.

She seemed to take pains to make herself specially agreeable, and continued to detain me by various bewitching ways, which the sex understand so well how to practice.

Suddenly I looked up and saw Miss Worth walking with a gentleman. She was just passing us. Their promenade brought them near the spot where we were sitting, every two or three minutes.

I hardly knew why, but I could not bear to remain longer where I was, and at last I rose, impolite as it must have appeared, as if to leave the young lady.

Miss Edgerton rose at the same time, placed her arm in the most natural manner within mine,

13*

and we thereupon commenced our promenade. Of course, at each turn around the room we met Miss Worth in her walk.

I knew Miss Edgerton was playing me off. In fact she managed to seem to be saying something very confidential to me whenever we swept close up to "that lovely girl, her dear friend," Miss Worth. She kept on in this manner till I was forced to ask her to dance again, as the only way to ultimate freedom.

In the latter part of the evening, while Miss Worth was preparing to leave, we met in the hall.

"Mr. Powers," she said to me, almost abruptly, "will you be kind enough to answer me one question frankly."

"Certainly."

"Will you tell me if in any way I have given you offense."

"I assure you, in no way whatever."

"I feel much relieved," she continued, with dignity. "I should reproach myself forever, did

I even involuntarily do aught to offend one to whose——"

"I beg you to stop;" I exclaimed, "if it was possible for you to give me offense, which it is not, it would be by continuing to allude to a circumstance which you know was purely accidental, and which I pray you never to mention in this way."

Miss Worth looked at me an instant as if fully to fathom my meaning; the next, her mother's voice was heard calling to her.

She bade me good evening, with a hauteur of manner I had never before witnessed in her, and which led me to curse Miss Elgerton, almost audibly.

.   .   .   .

Shortly after this occurrence, as I was strolling up Broadway one afternoon, I stepped in at Brady's fine gallery of photographs, on the corner of Tenth Street. Who should I encounter there but Mrs. Worth and her daughter. The two were looking at some pictures of the last important battle, which had been taken in the field.

Mrs. Worth greeted me, as usual, very cordially, Miss Worth not in her accustomed, frank manner, but with evident reserve.

"Mary has just had some vignettes taken, Mr. Powers. I wish you had come in a little sooner; you could have helped us decide which were best."

Miss Worth did not speak.

"By the way, Mary, I wish to step across the street to Stewart's, to do a little shopping, and I will leave you for ten minutes to finish looking at the pictures."

"I have seen all I wish, mamma," said the young lady; "I would much prefer to go with you."

The ladies bowed and quitted the hall, leaving me in a state of chagrin not readily described.

What can be the matter? After all, have I been deceiving myself again? Am I destined all my life to be made the sport of my own feelings?"

Then my mind changed. "Idiot," I exclaimed mentally, "do you suppose the girl has no spirit? She will bear a great deal, because she feels grateful to you, but there is an end to forbearance. You have treated her ridiculously.

"Confound her gratitude (the mood again changed). I wish I had never incurred it. I wish—in fact, I don't know what I wish!"

I was interrupted by the sight of Miss Worth herself, who had approached very near without my observing her.

"I have left my parasol, I believe," she said, at the same time taking it up and turning again to go away.

"Miss Worth," I exclaimed. She stopped.

I approached very close to her.

"The other evening, Miss Worth, you put a question to me which I answered. Perhaps you remember what it was. Permit me to put a similar question to you.

"Are you offended with me?"

She looked for a moment very grave; then her countenance relaxed. Extending her hand, she said, with a genial smile:—

"Let us say no more about it."

I took her hand, and was pressing it too hard or keeping it too long, I know not which, perhaps both, when a hurried good morning was uttered, and the hand was gone.

.   .   .   .

The spring came and went, leaving me as it found me, still on the *sand-bank*, yet not discouraged, nor disheartened, nor discomposed in any sense.

I continued to study events and watch for the moving of the waters.

At length the summer heats began to drive the inhabitants to the various places of resort, frequented at this season by the world of leisure and of fashion.

I resolved to go with the rest. I will visit Sharon and Saratoga and Newport, each for a

few days. It will be in character with my new
position.

.	.	.	.	.	.	.	.

"I suppose you leave town soon," I said one
Sunday to Miss Worth, as we were going out of
church.

"We go to-morrow," she replied, "to remain
to the end of October."

"I hope you will have an agreeable time."

"Thank you. I presume you will desert the
city soon yourself."

"I may be absent three or four weeks, not
longer."

"Business makes slaves of you gentlemen."

"Yes."

"You do not inquire where we are going,"
continued Miss Worth, pleasantly.

"I should be happy to know, however," I
replied.

"We are not going to Long Branch," she
said, hurriedly. "I shall never go there again,
never. The very thought of——"

She stopped short, as if unwilling to trust herself with the subject.

After a pause, she continued in her natural tone: " We are going to make a longer tour—as far as St. Paul in Minnesota. Papa's health requires such a trip, and we are all delighted that we are to travel, instead of spending our time at a watering-place."

We had advanced quite to the street. Unconsciously I was listening, entirely enraptured, not with what Miss Worth was saying, but with her. For the first time I found myself giving way.   *   *   *   *   *   *

*   *   *   *   My gaze rested on Mary Worth with a look of undisguised love and admiration.

*   *   *   *   *   *   *

I extended my hand. "It will be a long time before we meet here again—a pleasant excursion—good-bye ! "

It was well over—the next moment I was walking rapidly toward my hotel.

"The end of October," I muttered. "Before that time I shall be settled at what will tell here, or have quitted New York altogether—which?"

CHAPTER XXXI.

My reputation for wealth, business capacity, and extraordinary financial ability, increased in spite of myself—while I was really doing nothing at all!

This very consideration made me the more fixed in my resolution to leave the city, and go where I might commence in a small way, if I could not engage in something which should prove a decisive, if not a brilliant, success.

Although gold had now reached one hundred and twenty-five, the various departments of merchandise were still to an extent uninfluenced.

In the tremendous stagnation of the previous year, prices had sunk to about one-half their usual standard, from which they were slowly recovering.

I had conversed a great deal with my friend

Holman on the subject, which, of course, he thoroughly understood. He would frequently remark: "Now is just the time to commence again, if I had the capital." His wife often urged him to go once more into business, offering her own little fortune to aid him in doing so, but he persistently refused to accept it.

There really was nothing to prevent, for the energetic Mr. Gardner had returned from Europe, having arranged a favorable compromise with the creditors of the firm of Gardner, Lynde & Co., by which all the partners were free. He, Mr. Gardner, was already preparing to go on again under the firm of Gardner & Co. This house has now resumed its former position; indeed, many consider it stronger than it was before it suspended.

Day after day Holman and I would talk over matters, and always with the same opinion expressed by him—to wit, a certainty of a great rise in prices and in gold.

At length I departed for Sharon. It was

very agreeable, for I found many acquaintances there, but I was nervous and ill at ease all the time.

It seemed as if my destiny would soon take its ultimate earthly shape, and that I ought to be back in town.

I staid but four days at Sharon, and left for Saratoga, a good deal to the regret, as I was vain enough to imagine, of the pretty and fascinating Miss Edgerton, of whom I have already spoken, whose father was rich to repletion, and she an only child.

Yes, reader, on my honor, I think I might have proposed to Emily Edgerton, and been accepted. But had no Mary Worth existed, I could not have offered myself under a false pretense.

Besides, I never would have married a rich girl while I myself was poor.

At Saratoga I mixed promiscuously with the great crowd, but could find no enjoyment there, none whatever.

On the third day after my arrival (it was Saturday), Mr. Stokes came up from New York to spend Sunday. We had always been on very pleasant terms from the time I called at his house to endeavor to enlist him in the Coal Company.

Mr. Stokes seemed much surprised when I told him I had been more than a week away from New York.

"You must have left your matters snug," he said. "The fact is, although one of us is always on the spot, I hardly dare be absent over night. We shall have extraordinary changes, don't you think so?"

"Yes."

"There will be a new element in speculation, which will take in every description of merchandise. This will make an active money market. You agree with me?"

"I do."

"By the way," continued Mr. Stokes, as we were sipping our sherry after dinner, " by the

way, I never saw your name figuring in connection with 'Hope and Anchor.' You know you
called on me about it. I meant to have asked
you how it happened."

"I sold out, warned by the expression of your
opinion. I had great confidence in your judgment."

"And I have had great confidence in *you* from
the time I discovered your name withdrawn from
the list of 'trustees,'" exclaimed Mr. Stokes, with
genial frankness.

I will not detail the long conversation between Mr. Stokes and myself that same evening,
and which lasted into the night, and which partook quite of the confidential.

The result of it was that after we had become, as it would seem, really well acquainted
with each other (those few hours were worth
more to me than years of ordinary business intercourse), Mr. Stokes said, very delicately, that if
I were inclined to undertake any operation requiring more money than I had at command, he

would make any reasonable advance that I might need.

I felt that he meant this, and I replied with candor that I would be glad to avail myself of his offer.

"Don't misunderstand me," he replied, "I shall seek no share of your profits. The safety and repute of our house are in this, that we do not mix up in other matters. We have plenty of money, and I am willing to go a little out of the way and take your judgment as to any venture you may make, since you once showed so much respect for mine. As to compensation, our commissions and interest-account will cover that."

.   .   .   .

Monday morning—it was a close, murky August day—I returned to New York, giving Newport the go-by for that season at least.

CHAPTER XXXII.

"Seward is buying up everything he can lay his hands on. I *know* it. His head man is an old and intimate friend of mine."

Such were the words of my friend Holman, uttered as a part of a long conversation on the very night I returned from Saratoga.

"And yet Edward won't venture," said his wife, who had been a quiet listener to our confab, "Edward won't venture a penny, although I have begged him to take five thousand of my 7-30's and try something."

"It is true, Powers, I will not do it. I must not, I dare not do it," said Holman, firmly.

"Wait a little and we will see whether you will or not," I said. "For the present, it is, perhaps, well to say 'no.' For the future we will not commit ourselves."

" Now that is sensible," said Mrs. Holman.
"After this I shall consult with you, Mr. Powers."

"Agreed; and now I must say good night."

I went home and slept little. I thought
much.

The next day—I shall never forget it, for it
was one of the most sultry and disagreeable of
the whole summer—I took a solitary walk
through the east part of the town, or rather
through that portion of it where the small cheap
dry-goods men congregate.

Occasionally I would stop into a store and
make some trifling purchase.

" Business is very dull;" that was the general
observation.

One man whom I encountered, appeared so
much discouraged by the " signs of the times,"
as he called it, that he said he would sell out at
twenty-five per cent. below what his goods actually cost him, and would produce the original
invoices as a guaranty.

14

I told him I was about going into business, and after obtaining a further deduction for remnants and pieces that were cut, I drew up a short agreement, which we both signed, and I left, promising to send some one to take an account of stock that very day.

Returning toward the Bowery I perceived at the door of a pretty large store, the red flag of the auctioneer.

I went into the place and beheld, placarded around, in large letters, "Assignee's Sale." I recognized the young man who was to act as auctioneer, as a fellow-boarder in the house I lived at before going to the Grand Avenue Hotel.

He greeted me cordially.

"The goods will go for nothing," he said, in reply to some observation of mine. "Not a buyer here worth a row of pins. I wonder Lennox has not come. I sent him a hand-bill."

"Who is Lennox?"

"Between us, he is purchasing for Seward. I have it confidential."

"When does the sale commence?"

"Time is up now. The fact is, I was looking out for Lennox when you entered."

"Well, on this occasion I will take Lennox's place. I want to buy this stock of goods myself."

"All right, glad to hear it. Terms cash, you know."

"The cash is ready."

On this occasion, reader, I purchased nearly the entire stock in the store, and, as I have said, it was quite a large establishment.

The amount of my bids run up to eleven thousand three hundred and twenty-one dollars and forty-five cents!

I had in bank about seventeen hundred dollars. But, in addition, a fine magnetic frenzy possessed me.

I *knew* I was on the right track. I was certain of aid from Mr. Stokes, and I was determined to compel my friend Holman to strike now, for his own sake.

Before two o'clock I was at the private room of the great broker.

"I want ten thousand dollars to-day, and I may want ten thousand more to-morrow," I said, with a steady nerve. "I will bring invoices to secure you fully."

"Draw Mr. Powers a check for ten thousand!"

How easy it was done. How easy the way, if you can but once enter!

Confidence—confidence—it is the magic key which opens every door.

"Do not stop to make explanations. It is all right," said Mr. Stokes, handing me the check. "Just leave a memorandum with our cashier, and bring in what you have, any time before half-past four."

I went next to Holman.

I told him what I had done and what I proposed to do. "I shall go ahead whether you join me or not. But, for the sake of your wife and children, you must join me. Sell me every

It was quite time. The indefatigable Lennox —servant of the all-powerful [*in* "*dry-goods*"] Seward—had *felt* somebody operating against him in the cheap quarters.

Napoleon-like, he sought an interview with me, and asked me to say frankly how far I wished to go in my purchases.

"About forty-five thousand dollars," I said. "Certainly not over fifty thousand."

"Good, make your bargains. I shall neither compete or interfere with you. That is really all you want?"

"Yes."

Lennox even gave me some valuable hints which I acted on. And after that the field was left clear to him.

.   .   .   .

Reader, have you any idea of the price of calicoes? of shirtings, sheetings, muslins, et cetera, et cetera, et cetera? I am inclined to think you have. Therefore, you will not be surprised when I tell you that out of our purchases, Holman and I cleared over forty-five thousand dollars each, before the winter was over.

But I am anticipating.

CHAPTER XXXIII.

ABOUT the end of October, Mary Worth *did* return. How I waited for the event. How, Sabbath after Sabbath, I looked toward her pew with the hope that the excursion might have been for some reason shortened!

At last she was there.

It was the first Sunday in November. New York was in the midst of its glorious autumnal season. Rich colors were everywhere seen, in the foliage and in the superb dresses of superb women.

At last she was there.

I knew it because my heart fluttered violently.

Turning my head I saw the Worth family entering. I was certain that I should see them before doing so.

. . . .

After she was quite settled in her seat, Mary Worth looked, with a timid air, in the direction of my own pew.

Our eyes met—met as lovers' eyes meet. In that delicious moment all things appeared bright and clear, and perfectly understood. We did not look toward each other again, but each listened to the service with extraordinary attention!

. . . .

It is true I had not yet realized a fortune, but I was confident I was on the road to one.

Indeed, I did not hesitate to call on Mr. Worth, and say to him that I felt that I was now in a position when I might ask his assent to visiting his family, irrespective of any friendly claim on the score of accidental service.

Mr. Worth's reception of me was not merely cordial, it was appreciative.

I could scarcely realize where I was and what was being said. I seemed to live and move in some newly-created world.

14*

Was it possible? Am I to visit Mary Werth, with a full sense of a well-sustained self-respect? It was so indeed!

CHAPTER XXXIV.

How should I begin my courtship?

How did I know but, with the change in my condition, there would come not a corresponding, but an antagonistic change in Mary Worth.

[Women are such inexplicable creatures.]

Was it not natural to suppose that the feeling of gratitude which had been so persistently put before me, and which I sometimes hoped covered a deeper and warmer sentiment, might now fade away in the light of my prosperity, and leave me to commence the acquaintance, as it were, anew?

I feared this.

The fact is, I had not half the confidence I possessed when I saw Mary Worth in the distance. Then she was to me what his ladye-love was to each gallant knight of old, who frequently had no acquaintance with the object of his adoration.

In other words, as I came nearer my object, faith "further retired," till she was no longer in attendance to embolden and strengthen me.

What was I to do? should I pay a visit to Miss Worth, or should I wait for an accidental meeting to put in practice a more demonstrative course toward her?

I concluded on the latter.

It turned out precisely as I feared, in fact, expected.

We met at a little *soirée*—a very select affair—where I had an ·excellent opportunity to converse with her.

Strange to say she appeared shy and reserved —I began to feel so myself.

What had become of my assurance, my courage? in place of these crept in timidity and alarm. I now saw, as I thought very clearly, I had no right to hope that Mary Worth en-

tertained for me any particular regard. In short,
I had, like an idiot, taken it for granted that
when I was ready to pay my addresses, she
would be ready to receive them.

I passed a week in a very wretched state.
Then a reaction set in with an increase of confidence: so that meeting Mary Worth one day
in Fifth Avenue, I joined her, walked with her,
volunteered to go with her into two or three
shops on some trifling errand, and then accompanied her quite home.

On this occasion the time passed pleasantly,
but, alas, things did not appear at all as they
did when I had the whole affair literally to
myself — love, confidence, happiness, joy. For
I was my own creator, and could draw without limit on my hopes and wishes; above all on
my imagination; rarely, if ever, on my fears.

I will not prolong this account, nor tell my
readers of all the trials and perplexities (lover's
trials and perplexities), and doubts and fears
(lover's also), mingled with ecstatic glimpses born

of a passing word or glance from Mary Worth,
and which carried me along week after week.

Rumor finally began to speak, at first in
whispers of course, then louder, at last boldly,
and before I had dared to speak myself.

Yes, rumor declared that we were engaged.
Then everybody began to joke me about Miss
Worth, while she was the subject of a similar
badinage on my account.

Both of us managed to endure it.

The time had come when I had no right
longer to delay the crisis. I certainly had no
desire to do so, except I trembled at the bare
idea of what was possible—a refusal.

Could I survive such an event? Doubtless
I could. But there would be to me nothing
worth the surviving.

One afternoon I was passing Mr. Worth's
house (purely accidental of course), and saw
Mary at the window.

My resolution was taken. I sprang on the
steps, and rang the bell. A minute or two later,

I was seated near her in the drawing-room, where she was quite alone.

.   .   .   .   .

.   .   .   .   .

.   .   .   .   .

.   .   .   .   .

.   .   .   .   .

.   .   .   .   .

.   .   .   .   .

I have above recorded a true and faithful account of what passed at this interview, which must assuredly prove satisfactory to each one of my readers.

I say satisfactory, because each is at liberty to translate these mysterious little points into a language of his or her own. The matter-of-fact and common-place people (with whom I have no sympathy), and the romantic and imaginative class (with whom I have a great deal), will both be perfectly satisfied. Thus I shall disappoint neither the one nor the other.

.   .   .   .   .

.   .   .   .   .

"It was my destiny, I suppose," she replied, smilingly.

"And mine. Destiny hurried you to Long Branch where you say you had not thought of going till a few days before. Destiny sent me there after you. It palsied the grasp of the young man who held your hand, and strengthened mine."

.   .   .   .   .

.   .   .   .   .

"Nevertheless, I shall never forgive you for avoiding me a whole long year."

"And what is to be my punishment?"

"The thought of the happy hours we might have enjoyed, and did not."

"But *I* did enjoy them."

"How?"

"In thinking of you."

"I do not believe a word of it!"

.   .   .   .   .

.   .   .   .   .

CHAPTER XXXV.

WALL Street men will not be apt to forget the insane idea which took possession of the Government in the spring of 1864 to meddle with the gold market. Up to that time, gold had scarcely risen above 150.

There were true-hearted, loyal men in Wall Street, who did all they could to keep down the price of gold from principle. They had to contend, it is true, with the Southern monetary influence represented by certain foreign money-changers, and also against the "Copperheads" generally. But they did contend with them, and effectually.

Of this class was Mr. Stokes, and other names honorable, and to be ever honored.

When, however, it was definitely settled that Congress would undertake to interfere, sagacious men knew at once what the result would be, and acted.

In conjunction with Holman, who now was quite willing to follow my advice, I bought all the gold I could possibly command, with the use of every dollar we both had for a margin, and followed gold up from 157 in February to 285 in July.

It was a steady, triumphant, tremendous pull!

The moment prices began to fall off, we stopped; but not till we had cleared nearly two hundred and fifty thousand dollars apiece!

.   .   .   .

In the fall Holman and I had arranged our copartnership for a banking-business. The firm was to be POWERS '& HOLMAN, my friend declaring my name should appear first.

Fortified by letters from the President of the Bank of Mutual Safety (I no longer declined his aid) and from several other persons who were among the best men of the city, I visited London and Paris, and the various prominent towns on the Continent, where I arranged for correspondents, agencies, &c., &c., on advantageous terms. I need not speak of my subsequent success. The name and standing of the firm of POWERS & HOLMAN should be perfectly familiar to you.

.   .   .   .

Early in the winter Mary Worth and I were married.

I am a very happy man. She has proved herself indeed an angel of light to me, saving me, as I feel conscious, from a miserable fate. For, as I have confessed to you, there was a period when I was fast lapsing in the descending scale, and I think nothing but my romantic admiration of her prevented my sliding to the bottom.

Now what a change! On a sudden, I am lifted from a position which was wretched, precarious, and repugnant to my very soul, to wealth, station, and honorable repute: to more than this—to a life of happiness and bliss.

The only drawback, positively the only drawback, is the claims of what is called fashionable
life. The routine of that gilded world in a
measure enslaves us. It is hard to be deaf to
its flatteries and adulations—besides, I will confess
it—the soft and bewitching dream of worldly
prosperity in its first freshness has a great charm
for me.

．　．　．　．　．

．　．　．　．　．

What next?

You have my story. Extract what moral
you may from it. I can only say it is a true
history.

CHAPTER XXXVI.

"A WORD with you, before you go," about Wall Street. For by this term I designate the financial center of New York.

Few people out of it, really have any proper conception of what is going on there. Some have an idea it is a spot where immense fortunes are made with little or no exertion: others, claim that it is simply a large legalized gambling haunt; while a great many, even less charitable, do not hesitate to speak of it with coarseness as a "den of thieves."

There is a mixture of truth and error in these opinions.

In no instance does the proverb, "Things are as we regard them," so well apply as in one's estimate of the various transactions there.

One thing I will say. With the exception

of a small class of human spiders, who are
generally old men, and who in their dens lie in
wait for their victims, the vice of avarice—the
worst of all vices—is not fostered or encouraged
by a Wall Street life.

The contrary rather is true. For where does
a poor begging cripple receive so generous alms
as in Wall Street? Where does your needy
woman, soliciting aid for a sick husband and
young children, go with assurance of help so
soon as to Wall Street? Where is a tale of
distress so rapidly heard and so speedily responded to as in Wall Street? Where do people
seek for and expect the most ample subscriptions
to every benevolent scheme under the heavens?
In Wall Street.

But, reader, if you propose to enter the
" Street " as a combatant, and mix in its great
hurly-burly as an equal, all I have to advise
you is, make yourself up " hard." Keep yourself constantly under martial law; and, to quote
a single word from a favorite opera—*Tremate !*

P. S.—I had nearly forgotten to say that I have taken Deams into my employ as an outdoor man. He looks after the course of exchange, keeps the run of the foreign markets, and is very useful every way. He has removed his lodgings to Fifty-sixth Street, near Madison Avenue, where he indulges very innocently his love for a good dinner, a choice cigar, and a quiet evening. Deams has eschewed all former associates and associations. He appears to feel that it rests with him to keep up the dignity of our "house." It is amusing to see with what contempt he speaks of the "speculative class," and how he avoids any intercourse with people who are not solid!

www.ingramcontent.com/pod-product-compliance
Lightning Source LLC
Chambersburg PA
CBHW031338070726
47496CB00017B/1201